PUFFIN BOOKS

ROCK STAR

STAR

DETECTIVES

ADAM HILLS

Illustrated by
Luna Valentine

PUFFIN

PUFFIN BOOKS

UK | USA | Canada | Ireland | Australia
India | New Zealand | South Africa

Puffin Books is part of the Penguin Random House group of companies
whose addresses can be found at global.penguinrandomhouse.com.

www.penguin.co.uk
www.puffin.co.uk
www.ladybird.co.uk

Penguin
Random House
UK

First published 2022

001

Text copyright © Adam Hills, 2022
Illustrations copyright © Luna Valentine, 2022
Endpaper graphic © Shutterstock

The moral right of the author and illustrator has been asserted

Typeset in Baskerville MT Std 12/18pt
Text design by Mandy Norman
Printed and bound in Great Britain by Clays Ltd, Elcograf S.p.A.

The authorized representative in the EEA is Penguin Random House Ireland,
Morrison Chambers, 32 Nassau Street, Dublin D02 YH68

A CIP catalogue record for this book is available from the British Library

ISBN: 978–0–241–50597–7

All correspondence to:
Puffin Books
Penguin Random House Children's
One Embassy Gardens, 8 Viaduct Gardens, London SW11 7BW

For Beatrice and Maisie —
my own Charley and George.

★ ★ ★

PART 1

AMSTERDAM

☆ VIP GUEST ☆

VAN GOGH MU

DAY 1 – 6.30 p.m.

Leidseplein Theatre, AMSTERDAM

'Thank you, Amsterdam, and goodnight!'

Charley Parker bounded off stage with a grin from ear to ear. While most twelve-year-olds dreamed of being rockstars, Charley was living it. She had just performed to around three hundred fans (and some of their parents) in a beautiful Dutch theatre and, as she flopped on to a couch backstage, she could still hear the cheers bouncing down the hallway.

'That went well.'

Charley smiled at her best friend, George, who was half hidden behind his camera. 'Are you gonna follow me everywhere with that thing?' she asked, pretending not to enjoy the attention.

'How about a message for your Dutch fans?' prompted George as he started filming.

Charley tried to remember how to pronounce the Dutch for thank you. '*Dank je wel*,' she said carefully, blowing a kiss for good measure.

'Great,' replied George. 'Now let's go and meet them.'

'At least let me have a drink first,' cried Charley in mock exasperation. She picked up a bottle of sparkling water that was waiting for her on the table next to the couch, with a bowl of trail mix and some bananas.

She twisted the cap, and a torrent of fizzing water spurted, sprayed and spouted all over her, the couch and the floor. The bottle had looked innocent enough when it was sitting on the table, but it had apparently been transported to the theatre by a donkey trotting on cobblestones.

Charley stared down at the bottle and her hands, then up at the droplets of water now falling from her fringe.

'Actually,' she said softly to the camera, 'I might have to dry myself off before I do anything.'

Charley and George burst into a gale of laughter, in much the same way as the bottle had just exploded with an outpouring of bubbles.

When they managed to catch their breath again, George stopped filming and lowered the camera. 'Well,' he said, 'if that doesn't go viral, I don't understand the internet.'

He posted the video online while Charley looked around the dressing room for a towel, strands of her jet-black hair (with a purple streak) now plastered to her forehead. Unable to find one, Charley wiped her face on the only thing that was handy – the jacket belonging to her manager and promoter, Sam Mullane.

'That's my best jacket!' exclaimed Sam, walking in at exactly that moment. He grabbed it and put it on, grimacing at the wet patch Charley had left on the sleeve.

'I wish I'd filmed that,' said George.

'I'm glad you didn't.' Sam frowned.

A small bleeping noise came from the camera, signalling that the video had uploaded.

'Done,' said George. 'I titled it, "Charley's Bubble Trouble".'

Sam glanced at George, then Charley, then the puddle on the floor, and for a second he looked as though it all may have been his fault. As if maybe, just maybe, he had forgotten to buy snacks and drinks for

Charley before the show and had run to a nearby shop and back while Charley was on stage, shaking the bottle and causing it to erupt the moment it was opened.

At least that's what it looked like to Charley.

'Come on then,' said Sam. 'There's a foyer full of fans to meet.'

Charley, George and Sam made their way along the corridor and through the door to the foyer, where they were met by a throng of excited young fans. It was an orderly throng, though. A throng in a neat straight line. Charley had been warned that Dutch audiences were particularly polite. During the show, she'd noticed that they were quiet through each song – no interrupting whoops or whistles – but would burst into rapturous applause when each song ended.

Maybe that's what the sparkling water was doing, Charley thought. *Bottling it all up until the end of the show, then exploding.*

One by one, the fans came forward, introduced themselves and asked for a selfie. Charley obliged and made sure to say something positive to everyone who approached, like 'I like your earrings, Kimo' or 'Thank you for your Instagram post, Marlou.' She knew how much a kind word from your favourite star could mean.

Of course, wherever Charley went, George was

sure to follow, usually with his camera in hand. He perched in the corner of the foyer, filming at just the right distance to capture everything without making Charley's fans feel intimidated.

As the queue came to an end, Sam appeared at Charley's shoulder. 'Don't forget we've got that interview with Radio K-CAC for the US tour,' he said. 'We can do it backstage.'

'Oh yes,' exclaimed Charley. 'I nearly forgot!'

Although she had already posed with everyone who wanted a photo, there were still a few fans lingering in the foyer to catch one last glimpse of her: Charley Parker, the girl who had recently rocketed to stardom.

'Thanks, everyone.' Charley smiled. 'I hope to see you all again.'

As the group smiled and waved, one lone voice cut through: 'Thank you for coming to Amsterdam. It seems you made quite a *splash*!'

There were laughs all round.

'That was quick,' Charley said to George with a grin. 'Turns out you *do* understand the internet.'

George Carling focused his camera on his best friend and zoomed in a little.

Charley had returned to the backstage couch and was perched over Sam's battered old phone, which was wedged between the bananas and the trail mix. Sam always insisted Charley's phone interviews be conducted on speakerphone, so he could hear everything that was said.

'You're listenin' to Ronnie Dee on Radio K-CAC,' said a very excited American woman, 'and I'm joined live from Amsterdam by the one and only Charley P.'

'Hello!' said Charley.

'So, for our listeners who don't know, how did you become *so* famous *so* quickly, Charley?'

Charley flashed her eyes to George. Not only did he know the answer, he *was* the answer. 'Well,' she began, 'it all started when my friend George filmed me singing in our classroom one day, and posted the video online.'

George had first spotted Charley Parker across the schoolyard of Rokesbourne High School. One of the advantages of using a wheelchair was that sometimes he saw the world on a different level to everyone else. (This was also one of the reasons George thought he'd make a good comedian one day.)

While all other heads were turned towards the football rocketing across the concrete, or the tennis ball flying through the air, George saw Charley. She was the new girl, dark-haired (already with a purple streak) and wearing Doc Martens, sitting on her own and singing to herself. She didn't seem to realize anyone was watching her, and probably thought that no one cared anyway.

George cared. And he saw. And he listened. And, one day, George had an idea.

'Oh my *godddd*,' crowed Ronnie Dee from K-CAC. 'You guys sing in the classroom? English schools sound like so much fun. Do you know Harry Potter?'

'Um . . . no. I think he goes to a different school,' answered Charley, catching George's eye and grinning. 'And I wasn't actually singing during a lesson. I just happened to be eating lunch in the classroom that day.'

George could still picture the whole scene in his mind. The day had been particularly blustery and the wind had whipped up the students' energy like a mini tornado. Which was why George had decided to have lunch in Miss Fairburn's classroom. (Being susceptible to other people's energy was another asset he thought would make him a good comedian.)

When Charley had walked into the classroom, belting out a song George had never heard before, he hadn't been sure if she'd even noticed him – but he'd started filming anyway.

'*Heart thief*,' Charley had sung. '*You're nothin' but a heart thief.*'

George had been entranced by Charley's voice and presence. She'd seemed to become a totally different person when she sang. He'd wondered who'd inspired the lyrics, and made a mental note to never get on this girl's bad side.

'Did you know he was filming you?' asked Ronnie Dee.

'I had a feeling he might be.' Charley grinned, remembering the moment she'd caught George's reflection in the cracked window of Miss Fairburn's classroom.

'Did you get all that?' she'd asked, half smirking, half frowning.

'I'm sorry!' George had blurped. 'I'm so sorry.'

'Are you sorry for filming me or sorry for not getting it all?' quizzed Charley, as she spun round to face him.

'Both. No! The first one.'

'What are you gonna do with the video?' asked Charley.

'I dunno, maybe send it to the person who wrote the song and tell them you've stolen their tune,' George joked.

'*I* wrote the song!' cried Charley. 'So, if you send it anywhere, *you're* technically stealing *my* tune.'

She strode over until she towered over George, her hands on her hips.

Most people were too scared to even approach the kid in the wheelchair, let alone threaten him with physical violence. George was strangely impressed. Charley was treating him like she would any other person she'd just caught filming her without her consent.

'I-I-I –' stammered George.

'Either start rapping or explain yourself.' Charley teetered between a frown and a smirk.

'I really like your song . . .' George gulped. 'And I thought maybe you should enter it in the Too Cool for School competition.'

Charley was aware of the national schools online talent competition, and was pretty sure it had been named by an adult who had no idea how to talk to kids. *'Too Cool for School'? They may as well have called it 'Gettin' Groovy with the Whippersnappers'*, she thought. Despite the clunky name, the whole school was busy filming entries. The current favourite was Dexter Keaton, who was convinced he was the world's first hip-hop magician.

Charley hadn't been planning to enter. It wasn't that she didn't want to, exactly – she just didn't want to be rejected. Rather than admit that to George though, she just brushed it off as a stupid competition. Which was why George then suggested they upload the clip to YouTube, just to 'see what happens'.

Charley was snapped out of her memories by Ronnie Dee asking, 'So what happened next?'

'Well, we uploaded the video on a Friday, and by the time we got back to school on Monday it had five thousand views. By the end of the week it had reached over two million and a dance routine to the song had gone viral on TikTok.'

George grinned as Charley said all this, remembering some of the very first comments:

'OMG this girl is more talented than half the "singers" out there. I'd pay to see her perform live.'

'I want to be her.'

'Do you have an album? Are you on Spotify? Please do a show in Brussels!'

'So why do you think the video was such a hit?' asked Ronnie Dee.

Once again, Charley smiled at George. The truth was that her best friend had spent his entire summer watching online tutorials with titles like 'How to Maximize Your Social Media Reach' and 'Trending on TikTok' in the hope they'd help boost his future comedy career. George wasn't yet confident enough in his own material to post it online, but he was more than happy to use his knowledge for Charley's benefit.

'I guess people really wanted to see someone just sing for the sake of it, without competing for anyone's attention or using fancy gimmicks,' said Charley, repeating the words George had said to her at the time.

Sometimes it's easier to believe in someone else than to believe in yourself, Charley thought. And George really *did* believe in her. She was trying to be more confident, while also hoping that one of these days she'd manage to convince George to believe in himself too. After all, he did have a talent for comedy.

'What does a hip-hop magician do anyway?' George had quipped that day in the classroom. 'Pull a rapper out of a hat?' Then, turning to Charley, he'd become serious. 'You sing from the heart,' he'd said. 'And, when you do, everything stops. You're right, you don't need to enter a stupid competition, but your music should be out there for people to find. Cos there are plenty of kids who wish they could do what you do, and as soon as they see you they're gonna love you.'

Even now, sitting backstage in Amsterdam, doing an interview to announce her upcoming US tour, Charley still wasn't sure whether she was talented or not.

'I don't really know why people like my music,' she admitted. 'It's not my job to judge what I do. It's my job to put it out there.'

From behind the camera, George raised his eyebrows at Charley and gave her a thumbs up. It was their sign to remind her to be positive. She took his cue and tried to end the interview on a high note.

'I'm really looking forward to coming to America though! And to the rest of the European tour – I'm especially excited about the final show, back in London.'

'Why is the London show so exciting for you?' asked Ronnie Dee.

'It's my home town.' Charley beamed, back on track. 'It's where all my friends and family are. All this has happened so suddenly that it feels like a dream. To end the European tour and the year with a show in London will make it all seem real.'

George nodded and smiled. He could already imagine the look on Charley's face as she sang to a home crowd. That's when they'd know for sure that she had made it.

'OK! Well, it was so great to talk to you, Charley,' said Ronnie Dee. 'If you wanna see Charley in concert, you can get your tickets at CharleyP.com. Right now, though, this is her song "Heart Thief".'

As the opening bars of 'Heart Thief' began to play and the call ended, Charley and George smiled.

'Great job, Charley. I think we should celebrate,' said Sam, rescuing his phone from the table of snacks. 'And I know just the place – Freddy Fryday!'

'What's Freddy Fryday?' asked Charley, intrigued.

'It's a cafe serving nothing but fries. Fries with

pulled-pork toppings, fries with chicken-and-chilli toppings, fries with nacho toppings . . .'

Charley and George looked at each other with glee and said in unison, 'Best. Tour. Ever!'

DAY 2 – 8.06 a.m.

The Hilton Hotel, AMSTERDAM

Charley woke to the sound of sirens outside her hotel window. Weird sirens. Dutch sirens.

Sam had suggested they stay at the Amsterdam Hilton, because it was where John Lennon and Yoko Ono had held a famous 'bed-in' for peace in 1969. At the time, John Lennon was famous for having been in the Beatles, and his wife, Yoko, was one of the world's most celebrated new artists.

Charley wasn't entirely sure how spending an entire week in bed could bring about world peace, and she had a feeling those sirens weren't going to give her any rest. Another started blaring, and the sounds seemed to sync up into some sort of harmony. No matter where she was, Charley loved finding music in almost anything.

She got up, threw on a pair of jeans and her favourite AC/DC T-shirt, grabbed her key card and left the room. She knocked on Sam's door first and waited, but when there was no answer she crossed the hall and knocked on George's door. Again, no answer.

Charley's mum and George's parents had only agreed to let them go on the European tour on the condition that neither of them go *anywhere* without Sam.

So now what? Charley thought.

Sam wasn't answering, George wasn't responding, and Charley's tummy was rumbling.

She took the lift to the ground floor and went to the restaurant, where she spotted George at a table, his face obscured by his iPad.

Charley laughed. *If George ever commits a crime,* she thought, *I'll only be able to identify him from the nose up.*

'*Hola, amigo,*' she sang.

He jumped as if he was doing something he shouldn't be (which, technically, he was). 'What?'

'I thought you weren't allowed out without Sam's permission?'

'I thought you weren't either,' he replied with a wry smile.

'I knocked on Sam's door, but he didn't answer.'

'I did the same about an hour ago,' said George. 'I went to the park. Amsterdam in autumn is chilly!'

'So we *both* broke the law,' she whispered dramatically.

'I won't tell anyone if you don't.' George held out a hand for Charley to shake on it.

A police car flashed past the window, and yet another siren blared.

'Run! They're on to us!' George joked.

Shaking her head and smiling, Charley made her way to the breakfast buffet. She returned with a plate piled high with pancakes, waffles, doughnuts and a single strawberry.

George was both appalled and impressed by Charley's sweet tooth, especially at half past eight in the morning. 'Keeping it healthy, I see?'

'Ooh, how did that get on there?' she said. She removed the strawberry and placed it in front of him.

'Thanks,' he said. 'But, after last night, I won't eat anything unless it's on top of a plate of fries.'

'Ha! And I won't open a bottle of anything unless I can guarantee it won't explode in my face.'

'By the way,' said George, looking slightly smug, 'that clip has already racked up twenty-two thousand views.'

This is exactly why George is essential to my success, thought Charley. *He knows what people want to watch online.* In a world of flashy marketing and advertising, George knew that nothing would beat the power of one human recommending something to another human – especially if those humans were kids.

That was the real reason Charley had become so famous so quickly – the fans. She made a mental note to say that to the next interviewer who enquired about her rise to stardom. The truth was, most adults still didn't get the power of the internet in the hands of kids.

'I've put together a montage of our day yesterday,' said George. 'Wanna see it?'

He put the iPad between them and tapped play.

Snapshots of meandering trams, lemon pancakes and rows of wax-covered cheeses were followed by an image of Melly's Stroopwafels – the syrupy sweet, slightly crispy, yet somehow gooey Dutch waffles they'd sampled. George snickered as an animated 'S' appeared on screen in front of the name, making it 'SMelly's Stroopwafels'. Charley rolled her eyes.

'What?' he protested. 'You're never too old to make a childish joke.'

The montage continued on to the Amsterdam Duck Store, which was a shop full of rubber ducks. There were vampire ducks, sailor ducks, Harry Potter ducks, Sherlock Holmes ducks and the duck George had bought for Charley – the rockstar duck. She'd returned the favour by presenting him with the nerdiest-looking duck she could find. Like George, it was wearing glasses and a collared shirt, and it was reading – wait for it – a *duck*tionary.

Finally an image of the Van Gogh Museum, where Charley and George had spent the afternoon, appeared on the screen. There had been one painting they'd stood in front of for a long time. A *really* long time.

While everyone else gushed about sunflowers or bedrooms or Van Gogh himself with a bandage where his ear should be, Charley and George had been transfixed by a small painting of a simple pair of boots. The audio guide informed them that Van Gogh had bought the boots at a market and got home to find they didn't fit him, so he'd decided to paint them instead.

They'd stared at the old boots for so long that a security guard asked them to move on. Charley had joked that if the boots had been on sale, she would've bought them and worn them every day.

'I can't work out why I loved that painting so much!' George had said later, as they'd made their way to the theatre for Charley's show.

Charley thought for a moment. 'Maybe it's because we're a bit like those boots?' she suggested. 'Does that make sense?'

'Not really.'

Charley laughed. 'OK, hear me out. They didn't fit . . . and sometimes I feel like *we* don't fit either. But those boots were also full of character. They were cracked and flawed, but they were totally unique. And that's us too.'

'*And* we come as a pair,' George pointed out.

'Exactly!'

A photo of the painting appeared on George's screen now, with the caption: 'I want!'

As the video ended, Charley beamed her approval.

Yep, she thought, *I wouldn't be having half as much fun if George wasn't here.*

Watching Charley's reaction to the video, George allowed himself to feel a little bit proud.

Yep, he thought, *I do some of my best work when Charley's around.*

Like his invention of 'school-night shows'. Charley's European tour had been organized as quickly as her fame had risen. This had meant that, by the time Sam had tried to put together the schedule for the tour, the venues in each city were already booked up on the weekends. He'd slotted in shows on whatever weekdays had been available instead.

Thankfully, Charley's mum and George's parents had been happy to give their children a few days off school to fulfil their dreams. Charley's audience, however, didn't always have the same luxury.

And that's how the idea of 'school-night shows' had

been born. The gigs started at 6.30 p.m. and lasted for half an hour – perfect for an all-ages crowd. Charley's fans would get to see their new favourite rockstar in concert *and* be in bed by 9 p.m., ready for school the next morning.

'What should we caption the video?' asked George, picking up the iPad.

'How about "Amster-*damn* that was fun!"?' suggested Charley.

'Perfect,' replied George, typing it in and hitting upload. 'We're a pretty good team, you know,' he said, holding out his fist for Charley to bump.

Charley held her hand up for a high five, then wrapped it round George's fist as the two of them collapsed into giggles.

Their laughter was stopped in its tracks by a commotion at reception, where Charley and George spotted two police officers, three angry tourists and a bedraggled-looking Sam.

'Is he coming in or going out?' asked Charley.

'I dunno,' said George. 'Aren't those the same clothes he was wearing last night?'

'It's definitely the same jacket.' Charley snorted, remembering when she'd tried to dry her face with Sam's sleeve.

'Do you know what's weird?' said George.

'Dogs that look like their owners?' answered Charley.

'Definitely,' agreed George. 'But also . . . when I was out earlier, I could have sworn I saw Sam across the park. I yelled out and he didn't answer so I thought it was someone else. But maybe it *was* him after all.'

'Why would he be out?' said Charley. 'He knows he's not supposed to leave us alone.'

Sam spotted them and hurried over. Not only did he look like he'd been out all night, he smelled like it too. 'There you are!' he said.

'What's going on at reception?' asked Charley.

'No idea,' said Sam, his eyes flicking nervously from left to right. 'I was just getting a replacement key card for my room. Mine stopped working.'

George had about fifteen different questions. But, before he was able to decide which one to ask first, a waiter appeared.

'Would you like me to set another place for breakfast?' the waiter asked.

'No, it's OK,' said Sam. 'I'm gonna go back to my room and continue packing. See you guys down here at reception in an hour.'

And, with that, Sam was gone, although George noted that the smell lingered.

'That was strange,' he said to Charley.

She nodded, distracted by the sound of the kerfuffle at reception rising, now escalating to a brouhaha. 'What *is* going on over there?' she murmured.

'Those tourists are angry because the Van Gogh Museum will not be open today,' replied the waiter, still hovering near their table.

'So why are the police there as well?' asked George.

'They are the reason the museum will be shut,' said the waiter, as if that explained everything.

'I don't understand,' said Charley. 'Why are the police shutting the museum?'

'Oh, you haven't heard? A painting was stolen. A very valuable one. And now they must investigate.'

Charley and George fell silent, attempting to process both the news of the theft and Sam's unusual behaviour. All the while, the waiter remained in position.

'Would you like any tea or coffee?' he asked finally.

'No, thanks, we're fine,' said George, wondering why someone would offer coffee to a twelve-year-old.

The waiter still didn't leave. He apparently had more to say. 'Maybe a sparkling water then?' he said, adding, 'I promise not to shake it up.'

Wow, thought George, *that video really* was *effective*.

DAY 3 – *7.00 a.m.*
Goddard Road & Caryn Street, LONDON

Without having to open her eyes, Charley knew exactly where she was. Home.

She was in her own bedroom in the cosy house in north London where she lived with her mum. Charley had become famous fast, but apparently it took a lot longer to become rich, so Charley's bedroom still looked like pretty much every other bedroom of every other twelve-year-old across the country.

There was the desk at the window where Charley wrote songs, did homework and (more often than not) daydreamed. Pinned to a board on the wall was a photo of a tarantula (she wanted one but her mum wouldn't let her have one), a hand-drawn sketch of a tattoo (she wanted one but her mum wouldn't let her have one) and a page ripped out of a magazine featuring a girl with a pierced eyebrow (you know how this goes).

Charley took a deep breath, grateful to be back in her own bed. She had become famous for being a bit of a rebel, but she loved the comforts of home. If her life was a song lyric, it would be: '*I wanna rock and roll all night and snuggle up on the couch all day.*'

But snuggling on the couch would have to wait, because there was only one thing in her diary for today: school.

★

Less than a mile away, George woke up five minutes before his alarm went off, as always. He lived on the opposite side of school from Charley, but their rooms were remarkably similar: a desk, a window and a pinboard. The only difference was that George's pinboard had photos of The Comedy Store in London (he wanted to perform there one day), the Comedy Cellar in New York (he wanted to perform there one day) and the Melbourne International Comedy Festival (you know how this goes).

There was one other photo on George's pinboard:

a black-and-white shot of the jazz saxophonist Charlie Parker. George had once read that jazz and comedy went hand in hand, so he'd asked his dad who he should listen to. His father had suggested Charlie Parker, and George had spent the holidays soaking up his music, blown away by his technical skill and his ability to improvise. When George had discovered Charley's surname was also Parker, he'd been convinced that they were destined to be friends, and when Charley told him she was actually named after the famous jazz musician, George had felt sure it was a sign from the universe.

George surveyed his room, appreciating the sight, the sound and even the smell of home. It was an aroma (good or bad) that couldn't be described, but he knew it when he smelled it.

George rolled to his left and tapped a few words on to his iPad: *smells like home.*

Could be a comedy routine, he thought. *Or a song for Charley.*

★

9.05 a.m.
Rokesbourne High School, LONDON

In retrospect, George had known he shouldn't reply to the police officer's query of 'Do you know why I'm here?' with 'Cos you're having trouble finishing Year Nine?' The problem was, jokes for George were like sweets for most other kids. If he saw one in front of him, he had to take it.

It wasn't even as if Officer Neilsen had been mean. Although he had been just a tiny bit patronizing. You know, like when someone talks to you as though they think you're not as smart as they are. The way most adults talk to most kids.

The silence that'd followed had been punctured by the sound of a crunch, as the head of the school, Principal Haverstock, bit into a syrupy biscuit.

According to the plaque at the front gate, Rokesbourne High School had been built in 1897. According to George's estimation, nothing had been done to it since then. The school didn't have one of those fancy Latin mottos, but George was sure that if it did it would translate as: 'Bear with us. We're doing our best.' The buildings were in a state of disrepair, library books were missing pages, and after-school activities were non-existent. So many little things were broken that Principal Haverstock carried a roll of gaffer tape in her pocket, for any urgent patch-up jobs. Legend had it that she'd once fixed a leaky ceiling with only some gaffer tape on the end of an old hockey stick.

During a recent inspection she'd positioned herself in the doorway of Miss Fairburn's classroom as if she was casually leaning against the frame. In actual fact, she was making sure the inspector didn't notice that the door was hanging precariously from its last remaining hinge. The inspection had described the school as 'adequate'.

Even when she was trying to stop a door from falling on an inspector, Principal Haverstock looked like she was doing something official. George put this down to the Rokesbourne High School ID Principal Haverstock always wore round her neck, hanging from a fluorescent-yellow lanyard. (George liked saying the word 'lanyard'. It made him feel like he was on a sailing ship. In reality, it was just another way of saying 'fancy strap'.)

George was probably more aware of Principal Haverstock's ID badge than most, mainly because it dangled in his face whenever the principal leaned down to talk to him. He imagined that if you combined the lanyard, the ID and Principal Haverstock's upright posture from a back rigid with stress, she'd be able to walk into a hospital and start operating on a patient without anyone questioning her.

She's wearing a lanyard, all the nurses would think.

And she's standing so straight! She must know what she's doing. Here's your scalpel, Dr Haverstock!

George wanted to say all this out loud to Charley, but he took one look at the serious face of the police officer sitting before him in the principal's office and, for possibly the first time in his life, he refrained from making another joke. *An important part of being a comedian is knowing when not to be funny,* he told himself.

Officer Neilsen was so stern that George thought he looked like one of those characters in a crime drama who say 'There's been a murder in the village'. That's why, when the officer came out with, 'There's been a theft in Amsterdam –' George snorted.

Everyone turned to him. Charley had a sparkle in her eye that suggested she knew exactly what he was thinking. Principal Haverstock broke into a coughing fit so violent that it caused a chunk of biscuit to rocket from her mouth, sail across the room and land on the police officer's knee.

Officer Neilsen reached down, picked it up carefully and placed it on the edge of the head's desk, as if returning it to its owner.

'Oh, cuticles!' Principal Haverstock muttered to herself. George wasn't sure if it was her way of swearing or if she was admiring the officer's fingernails.

'OK,' said Officer Neilsen. 'Where were we?'

'Amsterdam,' answered Charley, attempting to play good cop to George's bad cop, in front of an actual cop.

'Thank you,' said Officer Neilsen. George thought his accent was Dutch. 'Two days ago, a piece of art was stolen from the Van Gogh Museum in Amsterdam. A painting of a pair of boots. The same painting that a security guard said she saw you two staring at and talking about for a suspiciously long period of time.'

Charley and George froze. Principal Haverstock retrieved the bit of biscuit and put it in the bin at her feet.

'A key card was found at the scene,' continued Officer Neilsen, 'from the Amsterdam Hilton. The hotel where you stayed.'

'Ohhhhh,' said George, attempting to look unconcerned despite the fear growing in the pit of his stomach. 'Now I know why you're here.'

'I don't,' protested Principal Haverstock. 'Are you accusing the children of stealing the painting?'

'At the moment I'm just following leads,' said Officer Neilsen. 'According to museum staff, the theft must have happened between 5 p.m. on the day of your show, Charley, when the gallery closed for the day, and 8 a.m. the next morning, when the painting was discovered to be missing. Can you account for your movements in that time?' He looked at George and Charley.

Charley knew full well that George would be formulating a gag about his bowel movements. She shot him a look that said, *I know what joke you're thinking of, but now is not the time to make it.*

George gave her a look back that said, *OK, but you know it would have been funny,* and kept his composure.

Charley answered first. 'We did go to the Van Gogh Museum during the day. But we left at about three, I think. Then we spent the rest of the afternoon at the venue, doing a soundcheck for the show.'

'Charley's a singer,' George added, 'and I film all her shows.'

'I know who you are.' Officer Neilsen sighed. His ten-year-old daughter was obsessed with Charley's songs.

Charley continued, 'After the soundcheck, we went for a pizza nearby, then back to the venue for the show.'

'Did anyone see you do all this?' asked Officer Neilsen.

'Well,' started Charley, managing to keep the sarcasm out of her voice, 'the roadies and technicians saw the soundcheck, the staff at the pizzeria saw us have dinner, and around three hundred people watched me sing.'

The officer cleared his throat, turning red.

'I can show you the video, if you want,' added George.

'No, no, it's OK,' said Officer Neilsen, a little too quickly. After hearing Charley on repeat at home every night, he wasn't in a hurry to listen to more of her songs unless he absolutely had to.

'So they can't have stolen the painting then,' said Principal Haverstock.

'What about between the end of the show and the next morning?' the police officer asked.

'After the show we went to a cafe called Freddy Fryday with my manager, Sam. Then we all went back to the hotel and to our own rooms,' said Charley.

'And the next morning?' asked Officer Neilsen.

'Um, well . . .' began Charley.

'What did you do the morning after your show?' Officer Neilsen pushed impatiently.

'Went to the park!' shouted George, at exactly the same time as Charley said, 'Slept in!'

'Well, which was it? You went to the park or you slept in?'

Charley's mouth had suddenly gone very dry, and George seemed to have run out of jokes.

Principal Haverstock was poised on the edge of her seat, as if she was watching a thriller in a cinema. Except this wasn't a movie, it was real life, and that wasn't popcorn in her hand, it was a biscuit.

'I went to the park on my own,' said George.

'And I slept in,' added Charley.

'So let me get this right,' said Officer Neilsen. 'The morning after you two visited the Van Gogh Museum, a valuable painting – *that you spent a lot of time studying* – was discovered missing. A key card was found at the scene, from the very same hotel you were staying in, and now you both tell me you have no witnesses to your movements in the hours before the theft was discovered.'

This time George didn't even consider making a joke about his bowel movements. In fact, at that moment they seemed to be brewing up a joke of their own.

George immediately pictured a number of scenarios, none of them positive: him and Charley being led from school in handcuffs; him and Charley in separate prison cells; photos of him and Charley on the news. His heart raced and his mouth went dry.

'But we both handed in our room keys at reception when we checked out,' spluttered Charley.

'Can you prove that?' asked the officer.

'No,' replied Charley. 'No one can.'

'Can't they?' retorted Officer Neilsen, before realizing that Charley had a point. Most hotels simply wiped the cards and re-used them instantly.

'Did you check whether the card found at the museum was for either of the children's rooms?' asked Principal Haverstock.

'Yes,' replied Officer Neilsen. 'Unfortunately the cards deactivate at 11 a.m. when people are due to check out and all the information on them disappears.'

'So you waited three hours before checking the key card?' shot the principal with a glare.

This policeman clearly didn't graduate top of his class, thought George.

'But there were loads of people staying at that hotel,' Charley said. 'And loads of people must have stopped to look at that painting that day. Why pick on us?'

'Because,' said Officer Neilsen, reaching into his pocket and pulling out his phone, 'you're the only ones who posted this.'

He fumbled for a moment as he attempted first to unlock his screen, then to find the post he was looking for. Finally he displayed George's photo of Van Gogh's boots with the caption 'I want!'

Charley winced. That post, along with the lack of witnesses to their whereabouts, made them look very guilty.

'That was just a joke!' said George.

'Well, I'm taking it seriously,' said Officer Neilsen. 'The theft is now the subject of an international police investigation.'

There was a whole bunch of things George didn't want to be: a poor student, a bad friend, a low-scoring answer on the TV show *Pointless*. To the top of that list, he now added 'the subject of an international police investigation'.

'I don't have sufficient evidence to take you into custody just yet,' continued Officer Neilsen, 'but I do consider you the main suspects.'

George couldn't quite believe he was in a

conversation in which the words 'suspects', 'evidence' and 'custody' were being used about him. He'd been raised to always stay out of trouble.

'I have a few more leads to follow before heading back to Amsterdam,' said Officer Neilsen, 'including talking to your manager, to see if he can vouch for your whereabouts. And I'm still waiting to receive the CCTV footage from the museum.'

'What should *we* do?' asked Charley.

'Well,' said the officer without a hint of sympathy, 'either prove to me you didn't take the painting, or find the person who did.'

'And what happens if we can't do either?' Charley asked.

'Put it this way,' answered Officer Neilsen. 'You won't be singing for a while.'

He stood, adjusted his belt and paused. 'I do have one more question,' he said gruffly. 'Can I get a picture for my daughter?'

'Umm, sure. OK,' said Charley, smiling weakly for the photo.

Officer Neilsen exited the room, leaving Charley and George with Principal Haverstock, who suddenly remembered she was indeed a school principal and not an enthralled cinemagoer.

'I'll inform your parents of what's going on,' said Principal Haverstock gently. 'I'd have called them sooner but this all happened so quickly.'

Charley sat back in shock. Two days ago they had been eating waffles in Amsterdam and promoting her US tour. Now they stood accused of an international art crime.

When she'd left home that morning, Charley had felt like she'd finally found her place in the world, doing what she loved.

Now she felt sick at the thought that her singing career could be over as quickly as it had begun.

DAY 3 – 10.15 a.m.
Rokesbourne High School, LONDON

'Did it hurt?' asked Vanessa Devine as Charley and George entered Miss Fairburn's classroom.

'Did what hurt?' replied George curtly.

'Being brought back down to earth,' said Vanessa, so proud of herself even her hair puffed up more than usual.

Vanessa had become the star of Rokesbourne Primary School after she formed her own band in Year Four. Naturally, Vanessa was the lead singer and, although the band also included Beatrice on drums, Flo on bass and Tara on lead guitar, Vanessa had named it after herself: Devine Intervention.

Their performances at the summer fair had been described by the *Rokesbourne Gazette* as 'obligatory'. No one had the heart to tell Vanessa that if something was obligatory it meant it had to happen, whether anyone liked it or not.

By the time she'd reached Year Six, Vanessa and her bandmates had amassed a small group of admirers, who referred to themselves as Deviners. Vanessa had hoped to carry her fame from primary school across the road to Rokesbourne High, and she was convinced that winning the Too Cool for School competition was the way to do it. She'd been briefly worried about Dexter Keaton and had responded by openly mocking him: 'A hip-hop magician? What are you – a rabbit?'

George had noted that Vanessa's attempted gag was nowhere as good as his 'rapper out of a hat' joke.

When Charley's video went viral, Vanessa became secretly snarky. As the song became a hit and the tour dates were announced, she graduated to selectively snide, intermittently irritated and then openly obnoxious.

The most recent insult came in assembly one day, when Principal Haverstock announced to the whole school that there would be a live music performance at the upcoming Rokesbourne Halloween party.

There were squeals of excitement. 'Oh my gosh, I bet Charley P's going to play! An exclusive set!'

Those squeals were replaced by an audible groan when the principal said the entertainment would be provided by Devine Intervention. That groan was then followed by a chant: 'We want Charley P! We want Charley P!'

Vanessa had been left totally humiliated.

George would have felt sorry for her, if she hadn't kept making nasty comments whenever she got the chance. *Did it hurt? Being brought back down to earth.*

'Not really. You broke our fall,' he said.

This was out of character for George. He had promised himself never to use his wit against those less successful than him.

Vanessa's face dropped, the rest of his classmates broke into guffaws (even Beatrice, Flo and Tara) and Miss Fairburn called for quiet.

The rest of the morning's classes were a blur for George. He exchanged the occasional glance with Charley across the classroom, while trying to look like he was paying attention. Mainly though, his mind raced about the case.

Was it a coincidence that the painting they had spent so much time looking at was the one that had been stolen?

'. . . fractions . . .'

Surely Charley wasn't the only visitor to the Van Gogh Museum to post about the painting of the boots on social media?

'. . . personal hygiene . . .'

But neither of them had an alibi to prove they weren't near the Van Gogh Museum on the morning the theft was discovered.

'. . . split infinitive . . .'

Every bit of evidence so far – the key card, the social media post, the time they'd spent in front of the painting, their different accounts of where they'd been that morning – made them look incredibly guilty.

George swallowed, sweated and shivered at the same time, while also wondering, *What was that bit about personal hygiene?*

★

As the bell rang for the first break of the day and the students congregated in the schoolyard, Charley and George made a beeline for each other. In fact, the line they made for each other was so straight that bees should probably start saying, 'I made a Charley-and-George line.'

Charley spoke first. 'What in the whatting what?'

George knew exactly what she meant. 'You've gone from heart thief to art thief overnight,' he said wryly.

'*Suspected* art thief,' corrected Charley.

'Suspected art *thieves*,' said George.

'Well, I know I didn't steal the painting.'

'And I know *I* didn't steal it,' replied George. 'Although I don't know for sure that you didn't.'

'And *I* don't know for sure that *you* didn't,' shot Charley.

Although they were half joking, each made a good point.

'Well, if we can't prove our innocence to each other, how will we prove it to Officer Neilsen?' George said.

Charley was defiant. 'We can't. So we'll have to find the culprit instead.'

'How?'

'We do what all good detectives do,' said Charley. 'We make a list of suspects, find a motive and look for evidence.'

George looked unconvinced.

'You're a pretty observant person,' Charley said. 'And you're better at storing information than anyone I know. And I . . .'

She was unsure of what she brought to the case, so George jumped in. 'And you're one of the smartest and most creative people *I* know, and you've got really good instincts.'

'I'll take that,' said Charley. 'If the two of us can become international rockstars in a couple of months, I reckon we can solve this crime in a couple of days.'

'Do you really think so?' asked George.

'To be honest,' answered Charley, 'we don't have a choice. You heard the officer – it's either that or call off the tour.'

The thought of their rockstar life coming to an end was enough to jolt George into action. He reached into his backpack, extricated his iPad and opened up a new note.

'So where do we start?' he asked, fingers poised.

'We identify a suspect,' said Charley, 'then we ask three questions. Why do we suspect them? What's their motive? And how do we think they did it?'

'Well, I suspect Sam,' muttered George, already typing the manager's name.

'OK then,' said Charley. 'So why do you suspect him?'

'Well, he wasn't in his room when either of us knocked that morning. I thought I saw him when I was out in the park, and we both saw – and *smelled* – him coming back into the hotel on the morning the theft was discovered.'

Charley nodded as George spoke.

'Plus,' said George, suddenly realizing something, 'he said he was at reception because his key card had stopped working. Maybe he was actually there because he lost his key card at the Van Gogh Museum, when he stole the painting.'

Charley had been taking all this information in and was now buffering like an overloaded computer. 'So what's his motive?' she said. 'Why would Sam steal a priceless piece of art? And . . . how?'

'Ah,' said George. 'I haven't worked those bits out yet. But it's something, right?'

'It's definitely something,' said Charley. 'In fact, it's all we've got.'

At that precise moment, Vanessa Devine passed them in a manner that could only be described as sashaying.

'I wouldn't want to be in your shoes right now.' She sniffed. 'Or should I say, *stolen boots*.' She underlined the last two words by raising her eyebrows, before turning her sashay into a departing saunter. An assortment of Deviners trailed behind her, giggling at her barb while not entirely understanding it.

Charley looked at George. George looked at Charley. They both looked at Vanessa's back, then looked at each other again.

'How does she know about the theft?' hissed Charley. 'And not just the theft – the specific *object* of the theft? It hasn't been in the news yet – I've been checking my phone all morning – and there was no one else in Principal Haverstock's office during the meeting.'

George had no answers.

'Well,' said Charley, 'put her name on the list.'

As George obliged, he asked the questions Charley had posed to him about Sam. 'So why would she do it? And how?'

Charley pondered this for a moment before answering. 'We all know she's jealous of me. Maybe she did it to take attention away from my show.'

'But how?' said George. 'By taking a day off school, flying to Amsterdam, breaking into the Van Gogh Museum and stealing a painting?'

'When you put it that way, it does sound a little far-fetched,' Charley admitted.

'Still,' said George, more upbeat than he'd felt all morning, 'at least we have two suspects.'

'But what do we do next? It's not like we can visit

the scene of the crime. It's in another country!'

Suddenly a message pinged on George's iPad:

> Need to see you both immediately after
> school. Usual place. I've asked Charley's
> mum along too. Sam.

The two students/rockstars/detectives faced each other and nodded.

'I guess we start with Sam.'

CHARLEY AND GEORGE'S CASE FILE

SUSPECT 1: Sam Mullane

Why do we suspect him?

Not in his room the morning the theft was discovered.

Looked and smelled like he'd been out all night.

Needed a new key card – maybe he'd lost his at the museum?

What's his motive?

???

How did he do it?

???

SUSPECT 2: Vanessa Devine

Why do we suspect her?

Knows a suspicious amount about the theft when it's not yet public knowledge.

What's her motive?

Jealous of Charley's fame and wants to make Charley look bad?

How did she do it?

???

When school ended for the day, Charley and George had one thing on their minds – interrogating Sam. They were focused, sharp and a little nervous. Which may explain why they both jumped in fright when Miss Fairburn called to them as they passed by her door.

'Charley and George, would you mind staying back for a few minutes, please?'

With some trepidation, Charley and George joined Miss Fairburn in the classroom.

'It's OK,' she said with a smile. 'You're not in any trouble.'

If only she knew, thought Charley.

'I just wanted to set you your next assignment,' she explained.

Miss Honor Fairburn was Charley and George's history teacher. She was also their *favourite* teacher. When she found out her students/rockstars would be taking time off school to go on a European tour, she was almost as excited as they were. She was a big believer in travel broadening the mind, and had suggested they visit a place of culture in each city and write a report on something about it that they found interesting!

Miss Fairburn chose the Gaudí House Museum for Barcelona. In Dublin it was Trinity College to see the Book of Kells. In Copenhagen she sent them to the statue of the Little Mermaid, and afterwards they handed in a brief essay on the fairy tales of Hans Christian Andersen. When they visited Brussels, George made a special request to see the statue of the little boy urinating, known as Manneken Pis, and he and Charley wrote a report on the importance of humour in art.

Before Charley and George went to Amsterdam, Miss Fairburn had been quite insistent that they visit the Van Gogh Museum. She told them to take their time savouring the pieces of art that spoke to them.

She even mentioned the painting of the old boots.

Now Miss Fairburn was scanning a handwritten diary of cities and dates. 'According to the dates Sam sent me, you'll be in Rome next week,' she said. 'So I'm sending you to the Colosseum. The Colosseum itself is an amphitheatre, but it also contains a museum with some rather exciting artefacts.'

Charley wasn't sure that 'exciting' was the word she'd use, but she let Miss Fairburn continue.

'In particular, I'd like you to hunt down information about an emperor called Septimius Severus. I think you'll both find him very interesting.'

Charley was about to ask Miss Fairburn why she had singled out Septimius, when she was interrupted by the sight of Principal Haverstock at the door.

Actually, she was interrupted by the *sound* of Principal Haverstock at the door, as the head of Rokesbourne High School accidentally leaned on the door, placing undue stress on its one working hinge. The door cracked ominously, threatening to break off the frame. Principal Haverstock lurched backwards into the hallway and, in trying to regain her balance, dropped her coffee mug on the floor. It shattered, coffee splattered, and Charley's question no longer mattered.

'Oh sh– shindig!' cried Principal Haverstock,

kneeling down to collect the shards of her mug while Miss Fairburn rushed over with a cloth to soak up the puddles of milky coffee. 'Don't mind me,' she said, as if it was possible for them to ignore the head of the school on all fours picking up pieces of porcelain, her backside facing towards them. 'I was just passing by and thought I'd see how my two international rockstars are doing. Has Miss Fairburn set you your next assignment?'

'Yes,' replied their teacher. 'I'm sending them to –'

'Ooh, don't tell me,' Principal Haverstock interrupted. 'I want it to be a surprise for me when they return.'

'I'm sorry about the door,' said Miss Fairburn.

'Oh, that's hardly your fault,' replied Principal Haverstock, as if it was actually Miss Fairburn's fault. 'I'll just add it to the list of things to fix before Tuesday.'

'What's happening on Tuesday?' asked Miss Fairburn in a hushed tone, as the two teachers got to their feet.

Principal Haverstock glanced over her shoulder at Charley and George, then motioned for the door to be closed. Miss Fairburn tried to do as she was told, but the door was now in such a wonky state that it only half shut, blocking the view of the conversation in the corridor but not the sound of it.

'The Board of Education are very unhappy with the state of Rokesbourne High School,' whispered the principal. 'They've given me until the end of the year to get it into shape. If I don't meet their markers by Christmas, they've threatened to merge us with Queenswood High.'

Charley and George gasped.

'What are the markers?' asked Miss Fairburn.

'The three Rs,' replied the principal. 'Repairs, reputation and records. I have a meeting with the inspectors on Monday to go over student records, then they're coming to check the state of the school on Tuesday. That's why I'm asking all staff to come in this weekend to help with repairs. There'll be an official communication tomorrow morning.'

'This weekend!' cried Miss Fairburn. 'But I –'

'No buts!' snapped Principal Haverstock.

George stifled a laugh, remembering the full view of Principal Haverstock's butt as she'd scrabbled to collect her broken mug.

'I need all hands on deck to help get this school shipshape.' The principal's voice dropped to a whisper again. 'We don't have the funds to pay for the repairs, so we'll just have to do them ourselves.'

An awkward silence settled outside the door, followed by the timid voice of Miss Fairburn. 'I have an idea of how we could raise some funds actually . . .'

'I don't need ideas,' the principal retorted. 'I need repairs!'

Charley wasn't sure if 'awkwarder' was a word but she decided it should be.

'While I've got you,' Principal Haverstock continued, 'we may need to talk to Charley's and George's parents about stopping the tour. I have a feeling it might start to damage the school's reputation.'

'No!' exclaimed Miss Fairburn. 'They – they have to keep touring,' she continued in a calmer voice. 'It's important to them . . . and to me.'

Charley and George exchanged worried glances.

'Besides, what harm could their tour possibly do to the school's reputation?'

If only she knew, Charley thought again.

Miss Fairburn's question was answered by the sound of footsteps, as Principal Haverstock strode off down the hallway.

Charley and George sat in silence. Eventually the door opened, and Miss Fairburn made her way back to her desk and sat down. She seemed lost in thought, unaware that two of her students were still in the room.

Charley noticed a redness to her eyes. 'Is everything OK, Miss?'

'I'm fine,' replied Miss Fairburn, who obviously wasn't. She was drumming her pen so fast that she could have provided the beat for a thrash metal band.

Charley wrestled internally over whether to probe further or to retreat into her shell like she usually did when faced with a difficult situation. She opted for the harder, better option.

'You look a little upset,' Charley said gently. She had once read that if you acknowledge someone's feelings, it gives them the chance to open up.

'I'm fine,' Miss Fairburn repeated, before sighing and adding, 'My mother is quite ill at the moment and

I need to find a nursing home for her. I was planning to do it at the weekend, but now . . . Well, apparently all staff have to come into school and help with repairs. Which means I won't have any time to go looking. Plus nursing homes are all so expensive. Especially on a teacher's salary.'

Charley felt a genuine pang of sympathy. Miss Fairburn had been so encouraging when Charley had first arrived at the school, and even more encouraging when Charley's career started to take off.

'Thank you for sticking up for us out there,' said George.

'Oh,' said Miss Fairburn. 'You weren't supposed to hear any of that. And I shouldn't have told you all about my mother either. Not very professional of me!'

'Is there anything we can do to help?' asked Charley.

Miss Fairburn paused, trying to formulate an answer. Before she could speak, George's iPad pinged with a message from Sam:

5 mins away. S

'Um, we really need to go,' George said hesitantly. 'We're supposed to be meeting up with Sam.'

'Of course,' said Miss Fairburn, snapping back into

teacher mode. 'Sam. Yes, a meeting with your manager is important.'

'Thanks for the assignment,' George added as he made his way to the door. 'I'm interested to learn about Septimius.'

'And thank you again for defending the tour,' said Charley.

'That's OK,' said Miss Fairburn. 'It's important you both know I'm on your side.'

DAY 3 – 4.00 p.m.
Whiskers on Kittens, LONDON

Sam Mullane, Charley's manager, was also Charley's mum's cousin and the keyboard player in a band called Rapscallion, who in 1991 released the novelty song 'Bouncy Bouncy Boing Boing'. It was one of those songs that made absolutely no sense whatsoever, with lyrics such as:

Do you wanna join, join?
Maybe flip a coin, coin.
Bouncy bouncy boing boing.
Hoorah!

It turned out no one in the UK, or the US, or

Canada, or Australia, or South Africa, wanted to hear a chirpy, sickeningly upbeat song with words that made no sense.

However, a great deal of people in Europe thought that 'Bouncy Bouncy Boing Boing' was one of the best things they had ever encountered, and the song became incredibly popular on the continent.

What Rapscallion fans didn't know was that Sam Mullane had nothing to do with actually writing 'Bouncy Bouncy Boing Boing'. Nor did he actually play any instruments on the recording of the actual song. In fact, Sam couldn't actually play any actual instruments at all, actually.

But when Sam's best friend, Marco, wrote, recorded, produced, sang and played every instrument on a song that became an instant hit across Europe, and was asked to perform that song live on tour, he asked Sam and his mates to come along and pretend to play instruments on stage while the actual music was played from a CD.

George often thought you needed three things to be successful in this world – talent, ambition and charm. George had the ambition to be a comedian but he didn't know if he had the talent. Charley had the talent to be a rockstar, but did she have the ambition? Sam had enough charm for all three of them.

When Sam saw Charley become an overnight internet sensation, he jumped into action, offering to organize a tour and manage Charley's career. He suggested they start by recording 'Heart Thief' properly in a studio and called in a favour from Marco to provide the music. Meanwhile George suggested uploading the song to Spotify (after explaining both 'uploading' and 'Spotify' to Sam). Sam then rang around the old venue owners he used to know and secured slots for Charley to perform.

Charley decided the setlist should be a mixture of her own songs and covers of some of her favourites, like 'Back in Black' by AC/DC and 'Seven Nation Army' by The White Stripes. But they all knew that 'Heart Thief' was the song everyone would be coming to hear.

'We'll get a whole bunch of posters printed up and plaster them all over town,' Sam had said with gusto. 'Then we'll send CDs to every DJ in the city, and finally we'll turn up with a stack of flyers and hand them out to everyone we meet.'

Sometimes it seemed as though Sam had flown in directly from 1995. Even George knew that posters and flyers weren't the best way to reach an audience of kids, and no one had used CDs for years.

'Or,' suggested George carefully, 'we announce the tour on TikTok and put a link to buy tickets in the bio. We could do the same on Facebook and Instagram.'

Eventually they agreed to do it all.

Sam presented himself as a successful and accomplished music promoter, but George noticed things from his vantage point that no one else saw. Like Sam's shoes.

Sam was very proud of his taste in clothes and often mentioned his expensive designer shoes. George had noticed, however, that the laces were slightly different shades of brown. He'd also noticed that the stitching on the sides was starting to fray.

And, while most people were immediately struck by Sam's head of thick black hair, when George looked up, he saw straight up Sam's nose, which was chockful of silvery, Santa-like nose hairs. This, combined with a tiny splodge of what looked like black hair dye that George had spotted at the bottom of Sam's carefully ripped jeans, suggested to George that Sam might be covering something up.

George had come to believe that Sam Mullane was someone desperately trying to maintain an image of himself that was untrue.

Now, as he and Sam sat in their 'usual place' in north London's only cat cafe, with Charley and her mum, George fixed Sam with a stare that was even more accusatory than usual. He'd never investigated anyone before and wasn't entirely sure how to go about it. Sam had plenty of practice in covering things up – his shoes, his hair, his apparent lack of money. Not to mention his short-lived career pretending to play the keyboard. If Charley's manager had somehow stolen a valuable piece of art, there was no way he was just going to come out and admit it.

Which is why George was extremely surprised, shocked even, when Sam's first words were: 'I've got something to admit.'

Wow, thought George. *This could be the shortest mystery in history.*

★

Charley loved cat cafes. As soon as she'd found out one had opened in north London, it was all she could think about. So when Sam had asked where she wanted to go to celebrate the announcement of her first-ever tour, she'd immediately suggested Whiskers on Kittens, and it had become their 'usual place' ever since. Charley loved the contradiction of being a tarantula-loving rebel who was also obsessed with cat cafes –

the rockstar and the homebody.

Charley was stroking a particularly friendly Burmese when Sam said the words that made Charley, George and even the cat bristle with excitement, nerves and fear all at once.

'I've got something to admit.'

Charley looked at George. George looked at Charley. Charley's mum looked at her watch, aware that she needed to be back at work in fifteen minutes.

'When we were in Amsterdam . . .' Sam began nervously.

Charley and George shuffled towards the edge of their seats.

'. . . the morning after the concert . . .'

More shuffling.

'. . . I did something stupid.'

Charley and George were now balanced precariously on the very edge of their seats.

'I'm afraid I, um, well . . .'

Charley wasn't sure how much further she could shuffle.

Then Sam blurted out, 'I slept in. I didn't take Charley and George down to breakfast.'

Charley fell off her seat, sending the Burmese flying and very

nearly injuring an unsuspecting Persian.

'Charley!' shouted her mum, in that way that parents sometimes shout when they are genuinely concerned for their child's welfare but for some reason sound really angry.

As Charley clambered back on to her seat, her mum fixed Sam with a steely gaze. 'So you're telling me the kids went hungry?' Charley's mum was a stickler for a good breakfast.

'No,' replied Sam. 'They had breakfast on their own in the restaurant.'

Charley's mum mulled over this information, as did Charley and George.

'I'm so sorry,' pleaded Sam. 'As soon as I woke up, I went straight downstairs to find them. I knew they'd be in the restaurant. They're very responsible, you know. But I've been feeling terrible about it. I promised I'd stay with them at all times.'

A spritely Siamese nestled into Charley's legs as Charley's mum sipped her cattuccino pensively.

Charley guessed it was possible that Sam had indeed slept in, woken up in a panic, raced downstairs to try to find her and George, then gone outside looking for them. Maybe that's why he'd looked so frazzled in the hotel foyer.

Something didn't seem right though, and she could tell George felt the same way. He wore the same look when someone didn't tell a joke right. Like the time Vanessa had said, 'Did you hear about the duck that went to the chemist to buy some lip balm? He told the chemist to put it on his beak.'

Some people laughed, mainly because of the absurd image of a chemist applying lip balm to a duck's beak. But George had known the punchline should have been 'He told the chemist to put it on his *bill*'. So, while everyone chuckled, George had looked on, perturbed, annoyed and a little confused. Much like he looked now.

Before Charley or George could form a sentence, or even an opinion, Charley's mum spoke up. 'Well, I'm proud of you both. You had the presence of mind to get yourselves up, go down to the restaurant and make sure you got a hearty and healthy start to the day.'

Little did she know about the pancakes, waffles and doughnuts.

'I am slightly concerned,' continued Charley's mum, turning her attention back to Sam, 'that the children ended up wandering the hallways on their own. What if one of them had left the hotel?'

At this point, Charley heard a tiny squeak come

from George's direction. It sounded as if a weeny bit of air had escaped from a tyre on George's wheelchair, but it was also possible it had escaped from George himself. Either way, she didn't dare look at him.

'I promise you, neither of them left the hotel without me at any point,' said Sam, casting George a sideways glance that could have meant any number of things. 'I'm really sorry. But, on the bright side, it did prove how responsible the kids are.'

Now Charley was conflicted. Should she ask why Sam had been at reception? Or why George thought he'd seen Sam outside the hotel? Should she admit she had eaten mainly sugar for breakfast? Or should she stay quiet and let her mum remain convinced that it was all a harmless accident that actually demonstrated how mature she and George could be?

Easy choice.

'Hmm, maybe you should all stay in an apartment next time,' Charley's mum pondered. 'That way, if you sleep in, they can easily help themselves to breakfast.'

'That is an excellent idea,' said Sam, turning the charm back up to eleven. 'You always were the smart one in the family, Grace.'

Charley's mum smiled.

Even she isn't immune to Sam's flattery, George thought.

'Plus it'll save us a bit of money too,' she added, 'which is handy. I mean, we do want the kids to end this tour with *something* in the bank.'

This last sentence was directed at Sam and almost certainly referred to his lack of financial security at the end of the Rapscallion tour.

'Well,' Sam spouted suddenly, 'that's all that then!'

Charley's mum glanced at her watch again. 'Goodness, I need to get back to work.' Her chair squealed on the ground as she stood, making the Siamese scarper.

'I'll walk you out,' said Sam.

'See you at home,' said Charley's mum, placing a kiss on her daughter's cheek.

'What about me?' asked George mischievously.

'You can go to your own home,' replied Charley's mum with a wink.

Once the adults were out of earshot, Charley spoke. 'Something's not right.'

'I agree,' said George, 'but I can't work out what it is.'

'I mean, he *might* be telling the truth,' said Charley. 'It is possible that Sam realized he'd slept in, then came down looking for us.'

'But why did I see him in the park?'

'You only *think* you saw him,' Charley pointed out.

'It could've been someone else.'

'Maybe,' said George. 'But, as you said, I'm pretty observant. Also, if Sam knew we'd be in the restaurant, why did he go to reception first?'

'Maybe his room key actually did stop working,' said Charley.

'Surely he'd check on us before getting a new card though,' said George. 'And why was he wearing the same clothes as the night before?'

'Maybe he fell asleep in his clothes?'

It felt so strange to be trying to unravel the clues of an international art crime in a quiet cafe surrounded by wandering cats. Charley absent-mindedly reached down and stroked the tail of the Siamese as it rubbed itself against her legs.

'Hold on,' said George. 'If Sam woke up and came straight down to the restaurant, how did he know his room key wasn't working?'

Charley paused mid-stroke. 'What do you mean?'

'Imagine you're Sam,' said George. 'You wake up, look at your watch and realize you've slept in. You knock on our doors and we don't answer, then you immediately come downstairs to look for us. How would you know your key card has stopped working? You don't need it to get *out* of the room. You'd only realize if you were trying to get *into* your room.'

'Maybe it stopped working the night before, when we got back from Freddy Fryday?' said Charley.

'If that was the case, he wouldn't have been able to get into his room *then*,' replied George.

The Siamese meowed at Charley. It could have been demanding more stroking, but it sounded like it was agreeing with George.

'I think Sam lied to us about his key card not working,' George said.

Charley gazed outside and saw Sam talking to her mum in front of the cafe.

'So why would Sam call us all together just to tell us he had slept in?' she asked.

'Maybe he wanted to establish an alibi,' offered George.

'What do you mean?'

'Well,' George explained, 'we know Officer Neilsen was going to talk to Sam. Maybe Sam panicked and made up the story about sleeping in. Then he realized he had to tell us the story too so that we'd all be on the same page.'

Charley picked up where George had left off. 'So you think Sam stole the painting, dropped his key card at the museum and made up the whole sleeping-in story to cover his tracks?'

Charley and George sat forward in their seats, ignoring every cat in the room.

'Go on then,' urged Charley. 'Write it down.'

George reached for his iPad just as Sam returned to the table.

'Sorry, guys, I gotta run,' he panted, grabbing his battered phone.

'Wait, we need to ask you a few –' started Charley, but Sam cut her off.

'No time to chat. I've got an apartment in Rome to book,' Sam shouted as he left the cafe again. 'Don't worry about the bill – I've already paid it. See you on Sunday!'

Charley and George sat back in their chairs. Once again Sam had left them on their own. At least this time they were only a few minutes from home.

'So what do we do now?' asked Charley. The Burmese cat had returned to her lap and she stroked it as she spoke, looking for all the world like a movie villain.

'Well,' said George, 'I say we go to Rome, do the best show we can, do some research on Vanessa and keep an eye on Sam.'

'Good plan,' said Charley.

The Burmese agreed.

CHARLEY P INSTAGRAM VIDEO

'Amster-damn, that was fun!'
96,975 views

Top comments
LeilaToomler O. M. Actual G. No way
Charley came to Amsterdam! The show

was amazing! Even got to meet her.
Aaaaaaaaahhh xxx

> **MarlouVR** I was at the show too!
> She said she had read my post.
> Squeeeeee!!

RebeccaG First concert I've ever been to.
Soooo muuuuuch fuuuuuun!!!!

> **Mimimimimimi** Meeee tooooooo!!!!!
> **Isaak C** Meeee threeeee!!!!!!

Loredana23 Anyone else heard the rumour
Charley P may be connected to a robbery at
the Van Gogh Museum?

> **FlorenceC** As if!
> **MarlouVR** You so fake.
> **MayZee** Loser.

PART 2

ROME

★ VIP GUEST

George Carling was enjoying the sounds and smells of Rome.

On this particular morning, the sounds were mainly cars, but George thought even their engines sounded Italian. Louder. More confident. Full of bravado.

A siren blared past. You would think that the signal to get out of the way so a police car or ambulance could whizz past would be the same in all countries, but for some reason it wasn't. *Maybe people of different nationalities react differently to different sounds,* George thought.

He was sitting at a table at an outdoor cafe with Charley (whose song was currently playing on a radio inside) and Sam (whose own sounds had kept George awake for most of the night).

The previous evening, the touring trio had arrived at the apartment to discover that it only had two bedrooms.

'But the booking form said three beds,' Sam argued as a young man called Paolo let them into the building.

'It does have three beds.' Paolo shrugged, his Italian man bun somehow looking cooler than an English man bun. 'In two bedrooms. One single, and one twin. Good luck.'

He sauntered out, leaving three sets of keys on the kitchen table.

'Looks like we're sharing, George.' Sam sighed.

George was OK with this, as long as Sam didn't snore.

Unfortunately Sam did snore. In fact, Sam REALLY snored. George spent the entire night listening to what sounded like a cartoon bear doing an impression of a cartoon pig.

As foreseen by Charley's mum, Sam slept in again, knowing that Charley and George could help themselves to the cereal, fruit and toast he'd stocked up on the night before. When he did finally wake up, Sam insisted they start the day by finding somewhere he could get a decent Italian espresso.

Why do adults drink so much coffee? George wondered. *It makes them jittery, gives them bad breath and, if it tastes anything like it smells, it's a wonder it doesn't make them sick.*

Sam had also insisted they sit outside because 'it was the best way to experience Rome'. Unfortunately the last time Sam had 'experienced Rome' was during the summer, and George was currently grateful for both his favourite warm coat and the outdoor heating.

Having devoured a tiny espresso, Sam started laying out the agenda for the day. When Sam pulled out his phone, George couldn't help but notice it was the latest model.

'New phone, Sam?' he asked.

'Yep,' replied Charley's manager with the faintest amount of swagger. 'Old one was a beat-up mess. I came into a little bit of money, so I thought I'd treat myself.'

'Oh really? Where did the money come from?'

It was hard to describe the expressions that crossed Sam's face as he tried to answer that question, but in order they were:

1 **Nonchalant.** You know, like when you casually know the answer to a question and are quite relaxed about giving it.

2 **Hesitant.** Like when you suddenly realize that what you're about to say probably shouldn't be said.

3 **Dumbstruck.** When you know you need to say something, but you can't say the thing you want to say, and you can't think of anything else to say.

4 **Panicked.** When the silence of you not saying anything starts to make you look really guilty of something.

5 **Fake nonchalant.** When you realize that your initial expression was the one you should have stuck with, so you try to plaster it back on your face while pretending that what is coming out of your mouth is completely natural and no big deal at all.

All those expressions crossed Sam's face within the space of about five seconds, as he said the following: 'Oh, you know, I had a little . . . um . . . uh . . . I ah . . . Well, let's just say a couple of small things went my way.'

George exchanged a knowing glance with Charley. Could Sam have sold a stolen painting in the past week? Was that where the money came from?

'Anyway,' Sam said quickly, 'there are still a few tickets left for tonight's concert, so Charley has a couple of radio interviews this afternoon. Before that, though, we are booked in for a tour of the Colosseum, courtesy of Miss Fairburn!'

Sam's phone rang, punctuating his sentence, and he immediately left the table to answer it.

'Did you hear that?' whispered George, knowing full well that Charley had. 'He came into some money cos a couple of small things went his way!'

'Write it down,' said Charley.

George pulled his iPad from his backpack and began to type, while Charley nibbled on a biscotto. The cafe had plenty of sweet treats to choose from, but biscotti was the only one that Charley had felt confident pronouncing.

The final notes of 'Heart Thief' drifted outside,

and they heard an Italian DJ saying a few words that included 'Charley Parker' and '*concerto a Roma!*'. The DJ then introduced the next track as 'Mambo Salentino' by Boomdabash with Alessandra Amoroso.

As the song began, first Charley's then George's ears pricked up in recognition. Something about it sounded familiar.

The moment the chorus started, the two friends erupted like volcanoes, spraying laughter instead of lava all over the footpath.

'Oh. My. Goodness!' shouted Charley so loudly that the man at the next table spilled his espresso.

George just shook his head. They had found the missing piece of a puzzle they hadn't even known about.

The very same song had been performed by Devine Intervention at the school Halloween party, but with English lyrics. Vanessa had introduced it as her own, newest composition: 'Mambo Seven Sisters'. She must have changed the words to make it sound like she had written the song herself.

What made them laugh so much was that the word 'Salentino' was so much easier to say, and sing, than 'Seven Sisters'. Even trying to say 'Seven Sisters' three times quickly was weird. Especially to a mambo beat.

'I can't believe she did that!' Charley burst out.

'I can,' said George.

'I always wondered why you'd sing about a north London suburb to such a dancey beat,' said Charley. 'I mean, nothing against Seven Sisters, but it doesn't really make me think of a sunny Mediterranean beach.'

'It's like singing a love song about the Arctic Circle. Or a punk song about butter.'

'Maybe *all* her songs are stolen,' said Charley. 'Maybe she searches the internet for foreign-language music that hasn't made it to the UK, then changes the lyrics and passes them off as her own.'

'That's a pretty good reason to want to sabotage our tour,' said George. 'Whenever we visit a new city, there's a good chance we'll uncover one of her stolen songs.'

'Go on then,' said Charley with a wry smile. 'Write it down.'

CHARLEY AND GEORGE'S CASE FILE

SUSPECT 1: Sam Mullane

Why do we suspect him?

Not in his room the morning the theft was discovered.

Looked and smelled like he'd been out all night.

Lied about his key card.

Recently came into money.

What's his motive?

Money?

How did he do it?

???

SUSPECT 2: Vanessa Devine

Why do we suspect her?

Knows a suspicious amount about the theft when it's not yet public knowledge.

What's her motive?

Jealous of Charley's fame and wants to make Charley look bad?

Doesn't want us finding out she's stealing songs?

How did she do it?

???

DAY 7 – *1.30 p.m.*
The Colosseum, ROME

Midway through their tour of the Colosseum, George was struck by how surprisingly accessible the Colosseum was for someone in a wheelchair. Sure, he'd had to negotiate his way over a cobblestone path at the beginning, but it hadn't been inaccessible – just really bumpy. Like when a four-wheel-drive car has to traverse a pile of boulders. Almost a fun challenge, really.

The rest of the tour, however, had been smooth sailing. There was a ramp at the entrance, a gate to the side of the turnstiles and a smooth, flat path all the way round the lower level.

Although George was pretty sure wheelchair access hadn't been a major priority in ancient Rome, he did wonder how people with disabilities had been treated back then. He had once heard a story about how the ancient Greeks used to value the opinions of people with disabilities, who were thought to have a different outlook on life. As if dealing with a disability made them somehow wiser, more connected to the world around them. George grinned at the thought of himself dressed in a toga, Julius Caesar kneeling before him, asking his opinion on whether or not Caesar's colleagues could be trusted.

'What are you smiling at?' asked Charley.

'Oh, just the thought of me in a toga,' replied George casually.

Charley snort-laughed. 'Now I'm picturing *both* of us in togas on our way to watch an event here in the stadium.'

George could almost see the two of them, wearing brown leather sandals, white togas and wreaths of leaves on their heads, meandering through the ancient columns and arches, about to join 5,000 of their countrymen and women to watch what passed as sport in those days.

'I assume you'll be feeding me grapes as we watch,' said George.

'Oh?' replied Charley in a posh English accent. 'I assumed you'd be feeding the grapes to *me*.'

'Actually,' interrupted Sandra, their guide, 'women and men didn't really sit together in the Colosseum. A seating plan was recently uncovered that showed the lower levels were reserved for important people of the time – most of whom were men. The emperor had the best view, followed by the politicians, then the businessmen, then the ordinary Roman citizens. The worst seats in the house were reserved for women and the poor.'

Charley and George pulled faces. Women weren't

even considered 'ordinary citizens' – and Sandra hadn't mentioned people with disabilities whatsoever. Were they even allowed into the Colosseum?

Unaware of the unease she had created, or perhaps in order to compensate for it, Sandra bounded on to her next topic. 'Oh, look. This is where the wild animals were kept before they were released into the arena.'

'Awesome,' exclaimed Sam. Until then he'd been distractedly scrolling and tapping on his new phone.

They were now under what would have been the floor of the stadium, and in front of them was a complicated array of wooden boxes, ramps and pulleys.

'This entire area would have been filled with cages,' said Sandra, 'ready to be raised up through the floor of the stadium. All kinds of animals would have been released, then hunted for sport. People in Rome never saw elephants, tigers and giraffes, so it was quite the big deal to suddenly see them up close.'

'It sounds a bit brutal,' said George.

'Oh, that was nothing,' their guide continued. 'In ancient Rome, if a person was sentenced to death for committing a crime, they would be sent into the arena with the wild animals and people would watch them being ripped apart. Of course, the main events were the gladiator fights. Maybe you have seen them in the movies?' She looked at Sam. 'These men would be trained in combat, given weapons and armour, and sent into battle in front of an entire arena. It was quite the spectacle!' she added cheerfully.

'Did all the entertainment involve someone, or something, being killed?' asked George.

'Oh no,' replied Sandra. 'There were also acrobats and magicians. They would keep the crowd entertained while the blood and entrails were cleared away for the next act.'

George gulped. Charley looked as though she was going to be sick. But Sam flashed one of his charming smiles, so Sandra continued. 'Sometimes even the emperor would get involved. It is said that Commodus would actually come to the arena and fight gladiators himself. But he was no good at combat so he would only battle men who were, how do you say, *non abilitato*. That way he knew he would win.'

George bristled. 'Do you mean *disabled*?' he asked hesitantly.

Blissfully unaware, Sandra answered as if she was describing her favourite meal. 'Yes. Commodus would choose men from the war – soldiers who had lost arms or legs. Sometimes he would make little people fight each other for the crowd's entertainment. But mainly he would do the fighting. Against men with disabilities. So that he would win.'

Wow. Just, wow, thought George. *People with disabilities were so low on the rungs in ancient Rome that a cowardly emperor would fight them to make himself look like a hero.*

Suddenly those bumpy cobblestones didn't seem quite so bad.

Sandra finally picked up on the atmosphere she had created. 'But don't worry.' She laughed. 'We don't do that any more. In fact, these days we even have a lift so you can get to the next level. Would you like to try it?'

'As long as the lift doesn't take me up to the floor of the arena, where I have to fight an able-bodied guy holding a sword,' cracked George, flashing Charley a grin.

Sandra looked awkward and Sam pretended to be distracted by his phone again. Charley laughed and the sound echoed through the ancient columns, making George think this part of the Colosseum would have made the perfect underground comedy club. He imagined an old guy in a toga telling jokes to the people about to be hoisted up to their deaths. *So how did the lion feel after he killed the emperor's wife?* Glad-he-ate-her! *Thank you, you've been a wonderful audience. Enjoy the bloodbath.*

Unfortunately Charley's laughter also caused all

the other tourists to turn their heads disapprovingly. A girl in her twenties with a nose piercing, a shock of red hair and a backpack stared at them a little too long, so Charley responded by poking her tongue out and the girl scurried off behind a column.

When the group exited the lift, Sandra led them to the perfect place to take a photo: a viewpoint that overlooked the entire stadium.

'Say *formaggio*,' directed Sandra, smiling at her own joke. '*Allora!* Now to the museum.'

George had been looking forward to this part of the tour. He was desperate to find Septimius Severus and see why Miss Fairburn had specifically mentioned the emperor to them.

'Woah,' said Sam, finally looking at something other than Sandra or his phone. 'Look at all this stuff!'

Before them lay a treasure trove of Roman artefacts: jewellery, belts, combs, cutlery, plates. All uncovered by dedicated archaeologists. All priceless. And all right there in an open display.

'What's to stop someone pocketing a few pieces, selling them to a collector, then using the money to fly away to a deserted island to live out the rest of their days?' Sam pondered, winking at Sandra.

Sandra blushed and spent the next few minutes of

the tour directing most of her attention towards Sam. Charley and George followed behind them, making mock lovey-dovey faces to each other. It wasn't until the two friends heard the name 'Septimius Severus' that they finally snapped back to attention.

'Tell us more about him,' George said enthusiastically, much to Sandra's surprise.

'*Si*, of course,' said Sandra. 'Septimius Severus was a Roman emperor from 193 to 211 CE.'

Charley and George gazed at the bust of Septimius Severus. Sculpted in white alabaster, it was an imposing sight. Curly hair topped a formidable face with a classic Roman nose. He had kind, wide eyes and a beard that was neat at the sides, but grew long and curly below the chin.

A smile crept across George's face. 'If you added a buttoned-up chequered shirt and bow tie, this guy could get a job serving up flat whites in a hipster London cafe,' he whispered to Charley. 'He'd probably still be called Septimius though.'

'What would the cafe be called?' Charley laughed.

'Rome and Away,' George replied, quick as a flash.

'Here is a painting of Septimius and his family,' continued Sandra, pointing to a small wooden plate. Unlike the statue, the painting was in full colour.

'Septimius was born in Africa, but his mother's ancestors came from the Italian town of Tusculum. When he was seventeen, he moved to Rome, and he actually spent his last few days in the English city of York.'

George was quietly chuffed to learn that the entire Roman Empire was once led by an African man who lived in England. Although George's family wasn't so much from Africa and Tusculum as Jamaica and Tottenham.

'Upon Septimius's death,' Sandra said, 'his two sons, Caracalla and Geta, were pronounced co-emperors and they ruled together, side by side.'

'How did that work out?' asked Charley.

'Not good,' said Sandra. 'The two men argued a lot and, after only a year together, Caracalla got rid of his younger brother, Geta. Which is probably why Geta's face is erased in this painting. It is believed that Caracalla removed the face of Geta from all statues and paintings – he wanted his brother erased from people's memories.'

Sure enough, while one brother's proud, youthful face gazed out of the portrait, a garland of gold leaves atop his curly hair, the face of the other brother was nothing more than a blur. It looked like someone had taken a scrubbing brush and some paint stripper to it.

'Is that why Miss Fairburn wanted us to study Septimius?' Charley murmured to George. 'Because his two sons turned on each other?'

'Maybe she's trying to tell us to always work as a team,' offered George hopefully.

'She chose a pretty bleak way of doing it,' replied Charley with a frown.

'Don't worry,' said George, smiling. 'I promise not to erase your face.'

'Thank you,' answered Charley. 'That's very kind of you.'

Once they left Septimius and his sons, neither Charley nor George paid that much attention to the tour. Instead, they watched Sam closely for any signs of suspicious behaviour.

'Notice anything?' asked Charley at the end of the tour.

'Nothing,' replied George. 'You?'

'Nope.'

But, as Sam handed Sandra some euros to pay for the tour, George thought he saw a phone number scribbled on the top note.

Alcazar Live music venue, ROME

When Charley Parker was performing on stage, nothing else mattered. It was like someone hit the reset button on her life: everything fell into place.

Charley didn't have the words to describe how she felt when she was singing, but, when she let her voice just flow, when she sang her heart out, when she let her light shine . . . it was like she didn't exist. In that moment, she was pure energy – no body, no thoughts, no worries.

It sounds strange to say that Charley felt most at ease when a few hundred people were looking at her but the truth was, in the glare of the lights, she couldn't see anyone. In front of her was just a beautiful dark, noisy mess.

In many ways, Charley felt the same on stage as she did when she used to sing to herself in the schoolyard: blissfully unaware of everything that was going on around her. Off in her own little world. Maybe that's why people liked watching Charley sing – they wished they could express themselves so purely and completely, free from anxieties and insecurities.

Of course, nobody would have seen Charley at all had George not filmed her in action, and right now, as Charley opened her heart to her audience, George was in his usual spot – offstage to Charley's left, filming both the concert and the audience's reaction. Often Charley and George would watch the footage afterwards. Charley would focus on spotting the reactions of people in the crowd, noticing the way her music made them feel. George would be hunting for the perfect moment to share on Charley's social media.

Floating. That was the word Charley was looking for. When she was on stage, it felt like she was floating. She floated through the after-party too, smiling as she posed for photos with her fans. And, even when the faces were gone, Charley kept floating for a few days afterwards.

Sam had said it was important to have a meet-and-greet because that was where you sold 'the merch'. In Charley's case, 'the merch' was a stack of handprinted T-shirts (made for free in Mr Brown's art class) with 'Heart Thief' emblazoned on the front and 'Charley P European Tour' above a lightning bolt on the back. They were pretty basic, but their simplicity made them popular.

As Charley said goodbye to one smile and peered ahead to the next, she noticed a familiar face lurking in the corner – a face Charley remembered seeing earlier in the day. The face of a girl in her twenties with a nose piercing and a shock of red hair.

The girl was staring at Charley again, but this time Charley returned the stare with a smile. The girl's eyes darted around the room, then she adjusted her backpack, twirled suddenly and left the room in a rush, almost bumping into George.

No wonder she was so flustered at the Colosseum, thought Charley. *She's a fan.* Most kids were happy to come over and chat in public, but maybe this twenty-something felt awkward idolizing someone half her age. *Is it possible that some people get* more *shy as they get older?* Charley wondered.

She wanted to run after the stranger and reassure her, tell her that sometimes the things that don't seem to fit can be the most characterful – like Van Gogh's boots. But then another thought crept up on her.

Could this person be linked to the theft?

Charley scanned the room, wondering if she was missing any clues. A couple of fans were muttering to each other, staring intently at their phones and then up at Charley. News of the theft in Amsterdam had broken on several international news sites earlier in the week, and George had shown Charley the Instagram comments from someone called Loredana23, suggesting she had something to do with the crime. Were the fans muttering about that?

Could Loredana23 be the backpacker with the red hair?

Charley took a deep breath and decided not to let the moment bring her down. She floated through the last few selfies then went back to the apartment, where she played a card game with George while Sam poked at his phone as if it had disappointed him.

When she eventually went to bed, Charley was still floating, now gazing at the ceiling and reliving the concert in her head.

Did she sleep? It was hard to tell.

Via Cavour, ROME

George had woken with a start, but he couldn't work out why. He stared into the pitch-black and listened. Something didn't quite feel right.

After a few seconds, he realized that the silence itself had woken him. The previous night Sam had snored, snuffled and snorted, but now there was no noise whatsoever.

George rolled over to face Sam's bed and strained his ears. Nothing. He grabbed his iPad from the bedside table and flicked on the torch. Sam's bed was empty.

Hyper-alert, George ran through the events of the

evening. He and Charley had played cards till eleven, then they'd gone to their separate rooms. George had still been awake when Sam had entered the room an hour later. He'd pulled the covers over his head to block out the light from Sam's phone, and he must have fallen asleep.

George tapped the iPad again. It was now 1.10 a.m. Outside the bedroom door, he heard footsteps. Sam must be having trouble sleeping too. *Probably all the espresso*, George thought.

Then he heard keys jangling, the apartment door opening, more footsteps, then the door closing. George sat bolt upright.

Had Sam just left the apartment?

He heard footsteps in the hallway outside the apartment, the lift arriving, more footsteps, then the noise of the lift again.

Was Sam leaving the building?

George's senses tingled. Then, three floors below, he heard the door to the building slam shut.

Sam had left the building.

George leaped into action. He found his clothes folded neatly on top of his backpack, put them on over his pyjamas and slid into his wheelchair. Shoes and socks went on next (not in that order) and George silently exited the bedroom, and then the apartment (with his own set of keys and his favourite warm coat).

As the door banged shut behind him, George thought about going back for Charley, but decided that would cost him valuable seconds. If he was going to follow Sam, he'd have to do it alone.

★

Charley was jolted awake by the sound of a door closing, then another, and another. She didn't remember falling asleep (does anyone?) but she must have. Had she been dreaming about being on stage again, or had she actually been on stage? Or was it both?

Charley groggily reached for her phone and checked the time. 1.18 a.m. She wanted to go back to sleep but knew she probably wouldn't. Her mind scrolled over the day's events – the show, the Colosseum, the strange girl with red hair – and she remembered George's words in the cat cafe: 'I say we go to Rome, do the best show we can, do some research on Vanessa and keep an eye on Sam.'

We've done two out of those three things, thought Charley. *Maybe I can do the third.*

Charley opened up her internet browser and typed in the name 'Vanessa Devine'.

A roll call of Vanessa Devines of all ages and

locations appeared on her screen. Melbourne, Glasgow, Indianapolis, Toronto.

How can I research her when I can't even find her? thought Charley. She tried typing in 'Devine Intervention'.

Did you mean divine intervention? asked the internet.

'No,' said Charley out loud as she clicked to reject the correction.

There was a book called *Devine Intervention*, a TV series and there, third on the list, was a Facebook page for 'Devine Intervention – north London's hottest music sensation'.

'Gotcha.' Charley clicked the link.

Charley scrolled down the page, not sure what she was looking for. There was a photo of a hand-drawn ad for their performance at the Halloween party, a clip of the band performing at the summer fair and a bio of each band member: Vanessa, Tara, Beatrice and Flo.

The page only had fifty-six followers, most of whom were Vanessa's family and friends, some of whom had left comments. There was one from Tara's mum, Fiona, one from Beatrice and a message from a man in a jaunty hat called Mark Devine.

Charley clicked on the name and was taken to the Facebook profile of Vanessa's dad. His profile picture was him in the cockpit of a plane, wearing a captain's hat. Below it his bio read: 'Husband. Father. Pilot.'

Wait, what? Vanessa's dad was a pilot?

Vanessa might not have been able to fly to Amsterdam to steal a painting, but *her dad* could have.

Charley leaped out of bed and ran to the next bedroom to update George. The door was ajar, so Charley pushed on it gently.

'George!' she shout-whispered. 'George!'

Nothing.

Charley used her phone to illuminate a path to George's bed. She tiptoed across the room, not wanting to wake Sam, and found that George was gone. Spinning, Charley aimed her phone at Sam's bed and found he was gone too.

The banging doors, Charley thought. *They've left the apartment! Sam must've left first, then George probably followed him.*

Charley ran back to her room, threw on a jacket and jeans over her pyjamas, pulled on her sneakers, grabbed her keys and left the apartment.

The chase was on!

★

The instant George left the building, he regretted it. Since the stairs weren't an option, he'd had to wait ages for the rickety old lift to come back up after Sam's descent, and it had taken just as long to go back down again. By the time George made it to the street, Sam was nowhere to be seen. In fact, there wasn't anyone to be seen.

George shivered. If his mum and dad found out he'd been out on his own in the middle of the night, he'd no longer be allowed to go on tour.

Mind you, if he and Charley couldn't find the actual art thief, the tour might be cancelled anyway.

George took a punt and turned right down the Via Cavour towards the all-night pizza place. He nodded at one of the customers as he passed, trying his best to look inconspicuous. You know, like your average twelve-year-old out in his wheelchair at one in the morning.

At the first intersection, George had a decision to make. He chose to head left towards the Colosseum. If Sam was doing what George suspected, that's where he would be heading.

George waited for the signal to cross (even with no cars on the road he still obeyed the rules) then made his way up the deserted Via del Cardello.

This might be the stupidest thing I've ever done, thought George warily.

★

Charley exited the building, looked both ways, saw no

one and turned left. She knew that she wasn't meant to be out, but felt like she didn't have a choice.

At the first corner, Charley turned right along the wide and well-lit Via degli Annibaldi. They had taken this road that morning, and Charley knew it led to the Colosseum, where it met with three other streets. She'd heard the saying 'all roads lead to Rome'. *In Rome*, she thought, *all roads lead to the Colosseum.*

Charley smiled politely at a group of people on a 'Rome by night' tour and hoped none of them had her mum's phone number. A couple of tourists looked at Charley with concern, and as she looked ahead she understood why. She was at one end of a long, empty street, at the other end of which towered the Colosseum. Would it be scarier if someone was coming towards her? Or was it scarier because it was empty?

Charley took a deep breath, steeled herself and kept walking.

★

As George passed the Colosseo metro station he could feel his heart pumping. This really was a stupid idea. At the very least he should have brought Charley with him.

When he reached the Colosseum, he stopped for a second to take it in. It was beautifully lit, even at this hour, and completely peaceful. No alarms going off, no one breaking in. No sign of Sam.

George felt a little foolish. And a little fearful.

He didn't want to give up the hunt, but he also desperately did not want to be out on the streets of Rome in the middle of the night, so he decided to turn left on to Via degli Annibaldi and complete a loop back to the apartment. *At least it's a main road*, he thought as he headed towards the corner.

★

Charley broke into a run. There was no one behind her, or in front of her, but she felt safer running. Ahead she saw a sign for the metro station and knew it was just round the corner. Somehow that felt like a safe place, so Charley ran faster.

At no point did Charley think there'd be someone coming round the corner from the other direction. She saw the shadow before the person, but it was too late to stop.

★

George screamed like a frightened goat.

He was face to face with a shadowy figure – the streetlight behind the person made it impossible to see their face. They stood over him, breathing heavily and quickly.

'George?' said a familiar voice.

★

Back at the apartment, Charley and George made themselves hot chocolates.

'Well, that was the dumbest thing we've ever done,' admitted Charley.

'I know,' said George. 'And we didn't even do it together.'

'So now what?'

George thought for a second. 'Well,' he began, 'we tried to follow Sam out of the apartment and that didn't work, so let's stake him out right here *in* the apartment.'

Charley made her confused Scooby Doo noise.

'Let's both keep our eyes and ears open for when he returns,' George explained. 'Be sure to take note of what time he comes back too. In case we need it as evidence.'

'Got it, chief.' Charley saluted mid-yawn.

Unfortunately the excitement of the day had taken its toll and within minutes of returning to their rooms, Charley and George were sound asleep.

One last thought crossed Charley's mind before she passed out: *Oh man! I completely forgot to tell George about Vanessa's dad!*

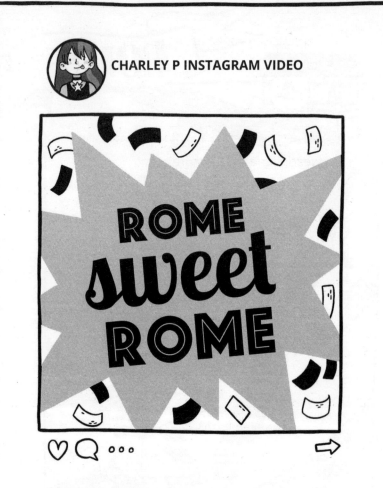

CHARLEY P INSTAGRAM VIDEO

'Rome Sweet Rome'

108,102 views

Top comments

RosinaV09 Bravissima, Charley. Your Roma

show was molto molto bene. You look so

happy when you're on stage. Kisses from Italy.

MiaCucina Can't believe it's been two days since I saw Charley P in Roma. I am still wearing the shirt. Amore. xxx

> **LeilaToomler** I sleep in my Charley P shirt every night!!!

Loredana23 I heard there was another art theft on the same night as Charley's show.

> **Acacia** What would you know?
>
> **Mimimimimimi** No way! Really?
>
> **FlorenceC** If it's true, it does look a bit suspicious.
>
> **MayZee** Loser.

DAY 9 – 9.05 a.m.

Rokesbourne High School, LONDON

'All right,' said George with mock confidence, 'we'll take the case!'

Officer Neilsen was dumbstruck, Charley suppressed a laugh, and Principal Haverstock bit down so hard on a little roll of pastry that chocolate cream shot out of the end and landed on her desk.

Once again George's instinct to make a joke had kicked in, despite the severity of the situation. Actually, George's instinct to make a joke had kicked in *because of* the severity of the situation.

The day after the show in Rome had been

uneventful. No alarms, no sirens, no stress. Charley and George had slept in – *a lot* – and were so exhausted from the previous night's events that they spent most of the day walking around like zombies. Without saying as much, the two rockstar detectives had decided to take a day off from being both rockstars and detectives.

No one said anything to Sam about his night-time disappearance, although Charley and George made sure not to let him out of their sight. By the time they'd returned to London it was hard to tell what had actually happened and what had been a dream.

The next morning, George saw the comments about another theft on Charley's Instagram post, but he dismissed it. *Surely if there'd been another crime Charley and I would have heard about it*, he thought.

Upon his arrival at school, however, George was immediately summoned to Principal Haverstock's office, where he met the familiar form of Officer Neilsen. George knew Charley would be late – she was always late the first day back after a show – so he took some time to rehearse the perfect line to defuse the tension. Something that would make Charley feel at ease when she arrived and take the sting out of Officer Neilsen's tail.

Which is why George had said, 'All right, we'll take

the case!' It wasn't quite the perfect line though, and he knew it.

'I beg your pardon?' said Officer Neilsen, finally rediscovering the power of speech.

'We'll take the case,' George repeated. He knew doubling down was a risky move, but, hey, if you're skating on thin ice, you might as well tap dance. 'You've got an unsolved crime on your hands, and you need some help tracking down the culprits. I mean, Charley and I are a little busy with schoolwork and Amsterdam's not exactly close by, but I'm sure we can come to an agreement.' George waited a beat before delivering his final offer with a tiny smile: 'For a suitable fee.'

The words hung in the air. No one moved. Principal Haverstock was still holding the pastry to her mouth with one hand like it was the world's crumbliest straw.

'I've just flown in from Rome,' began the police officer wearily. Yesterday morning a valuable artefact from the Colosseum was discovered missing. From the Colosseum Museum, to be precise.'

George noted that 'Colosseum' rhymed with 'museum' but decided now wasn't the time to comment on this.

'The cleaners said the piece was in place when the Colosseum closed on Monday evening, but staff discovered it missing when they opened up at nine the next morning, leading us to believe it was taken overnight.'

A thousand thoughts passed between Charley and George. They were suddenly back on detective duty after a day of rest.

'Why come to us about it?' asked Charley tentatively.

'A flyer for your concert was found three metres away from where the piece should have been.'

George and Charley looked at each other, thinking the exact same thing: *Those stupid flyers!*

Sam had never let go of his belief that flyers were the best way to promote Charley's shows. He had called in a favour from a friend, who'd designed and printed the flyers himself. Charley thought they looked terrible. They were too bright and too loud, and they made the concert look like a TV show for toddlers. It was exactly the type of design an adult would think a kid would like.

George winced at the memory of carrying stacks of flyers in his backpack in case he spotted anyone who might be in their 'target audience'. Sam thought it was a nice touch to be handed something by the person actually doing the show. Charley and George thought it made them look desperate.

Sam had even suggested that they hand out flyers at school, but neither Charley nor George thought that was a good idea. Instead they'd taken a single flyer to Miss Fairburn as a thank you for letting them tour. She'd seemed genuinely touched by the gesture and pinned it above her desk in the classroom.

The flyer later caught the attention of Principal Haverstock, who complimented the design. 'I don't suppose you've got a spare for your principal?' she'd asked after seeking out Charley and George one lunchtime.

'We've got plenty,' Charley had said at the time. 'It's not like we're actually gonna hand them out to anyone.'

She felt a pang of remorse as she realized she'd never actually brought in that spare for her principal. Now those flyers were coming back to haunt them – or, more accurately, accuse them.

Principal Haverstock rushed to their defence. 'Anyone could have dropped a flyer. I mean, how many did you hand out?'

George looked at Charley, who looked back at George glumly.

'None,' said George quietly.

The officer's head jerked to attention.

'What do you mean, "none"?' said Principal

Haverstock.

'We didn't give out any flyers,' admitted George.

'Well, this *is* interesting,' said the officer. 'Are you telling me that the only people who could've been in possession of the flyers were you two?'

'And Sam!' added Charley.

The police officer made a note on his pad.

Slowly and carefully he asked, 'Were you at the Colosseum two days ago?'

Softly and reluctantly, Charley and George both answered, 'Yes.'

'I see. And did you visit the Colosseum Museum?' asked Officer Neilsen.

'Yes, we both did,' said George.

None of this looked good, a fact confirmed by Officer Neilsen when he said, 'None of this looks good.'

'*Surely* you don't think the children are responsible for another theft?' Principal Haverstock said.

'There have now been two thefts at places the children have visited, and at each crime scene there has been a piece of evidence that links directly to them.' Officer Neilsen turned his attention to Charley and George, asking, 'Do you have an alibi between the time your show finished and the time the Colosseum opened the next morning?'

'Yes,' George explained. 'We went back to our apartment with Sam, and we went to bed around eleven.'

'And what happened between 11 p.m. and 9 a.m.?'

'We slept,' answered Charley. She wasn't technically lying – they did sleep. She just left out the bit where they woke up, left the apartment and wound up right next to the Colosseum.

'And can Sam confirm this?'

'Yes,' answered Charley and George in unison. They didn't look at each other. Technically they still weren't lying. After all, Sam didn't know they'd left the apartment.

'And was he with you at all times?'

'Yes.' This time they did, technically, lie.

'All right then,' said the officer. 'I'm going to go and talk to Sam. But if his story differs from yours in any way, you can say goodbye to touring until the investigation has been solved.'

'What did the CCTV footage show?' asked Principal Haverstock.

'It seems the cameras in the Colosseum Museum and the Van Gogh Museum were covered. It's likely that whoever took the artworks is responsible for that too.'

'What about questioning other suspects?' asked George.

The officer fixed him with a deadly serious glare and replied, 'Right now, there *are* no other suspects.'

George felt the blood drain from his face, and he imagined Charley felt the same. How could this be happening? He pictured the faces of his classmates, his teachers, his dad . . . His bottom lip began to quiver.

'Excuse me, officer,' he said. 'I don't suppose you happen to know which piece of art was stolen?'

'Yes, of course,' replied the officer, who had started to wonder who would play him in a movie version of the case, Zac Efron or one of the Jonas Brothers? 'It was a plate featuring a painting of the Roman emperor Septimius Severus and his family, with the younger son's face erased.'

George gulped. Now they really *were* in trouble.

★

'Well, that was dramatic.' Principal Haverstock laughed nervously, once Officer Neilsen had left the room.

Charley felt anything but flippant. Her career was about to be derailed by something completely out of her control. Worse, she faced being humiliated in front of the whole school. She pictured Vanessa, Tara, Beatrice and Flo leading the Deviners in a chorus of jeers and laughter at her cancelled tour, and it made her shudder.

Principal Haverstock seemed to sense the impending arrival of tears and busied herself with another pastry. Like the first one, it was a tiny rolled-up tube with chocolate cream inside. This time she was careful to bite more gently. She swallowed, then said, 'I think you should both head back to class, and, uh, try not to think about it.'

Strangely, this actually helped.

'Oh, and it's probably best not to say anything publicly about the thefts,' she added. 'We only just managed to take care of the repairs for the inspectors yesterday. Let's not say anything that could potentially harm the school's reputation.'

Charley looked at George, who nodded in agreement. The two left the principal's office together.

'Should we talk about this now?' asked George after a few seconds had passed.

'I think I need to process it all first,' replied Charley. 'Let's meet up at break time.'

So many emotions were bubbling up inside Charley that she needed to let them out. She wanted to scream. She wanted to tell George how confused she was, how scared she felt, how tiring it was to go from floating above the world to crashing back down again. But she didn't have the words, the time or the energy.

Instead they made their way to the classroom in silence.

DAY 9 – 10.30 a.m.
Rokesbourne High School, LONDON

Charley spent the rest of the morning in her own little bubble, but at break time she made her customary beeline for George.

'I wasn't sure you'd want to talk to me,' said George.

'I'm sorry,' said Charley. 'I needed time to get my head around everything.'

'And did you?'

'Not really.' She slumped on to a bench. 'None of it makes any sense.'

'Good thing you made me write it all down then.' George extracted his iPad from his backpack. He was just as worried as Charley, but he tried to appear calm to make her feel better.

'OK, let's recap the facts,' said George. 'The night we performed in Amsterdam, a Van Gogh painting went missing – the same painting we had looked at that day. The only evidence linking us to the crime was a key card from our hotel. Then, the day we performed in Rome, a plate was stolen from the museum we visited – a plate featuring a painting of the Roman emperor we were told to learn about. This time the evidence pointing to us was a flyer for your concert, which wouldn't be so bad if we had actually handed some flyers out.'

'So, who do we suspect?' Charley slowly straightened up from a slump.

'Let's start with our original suspect – Sam.' George tapped the screen. 'Mainly because he was the one who disappeared in the middle of the night, which is when the plate was stolen.'

'And we know he came into some money after Amsterdam,' said Charley. 'But how do we think he did it?'

'Ooh!' exclaimed George. 'I saw him give his phone number to the tour guide. Maybe they met up late at night and stole it together.'

'Yes!' said Charley. 'He definitely turned on the charm with her during the tour. And, if he was clumsy enough to leave behind his key card the first time, he's certainly careless enough to drop a flyer the second time. He had as many flyers in his bag as you did.'

George suddenly looked horrified. 'Or maybe Sam purposely left a flyer there to make it look like we did it. He could have done the same with the key card!'

'Wait a minute! Are you saying Sam might be framing us?' asked Charley, aghast.

'Maybe,' said George. Then he remembered he was meant to be calming Charley down. 'Probably not though,' he added too late.

Charley was conflicted. It was one thing to think her mum's cousin might be stealing the art, but it was another to suggest he was trying to make it look like she and George were responsible.

'What about Vanessa?' she asked, changing the subject.

'What *about* me?' came Vanessa's reply.

Charley jumped, then spun on the bench to see Vanessa behind her, flanked by her bandmates. Had she been lurking nearby, waiting to pounce at the sound of her own name?

George quickly hid his iPad while Charley tried to think of something to say, but Vanessa didn't seem to want a response.

'Hope you guys aren't in any trouble.' She smiled sweetly.

'We're fine, thanks,' answered George with mock politeness.

'It would be a shame to see the queen knocked off her throne,' Vanessa said snarkily. She paused a moment before adding, 'Or the emperor erased from the painting.'

She swished her hair, flashed a smile and sashayed away. As usual she was followed by Beatrice and Flo, but this time Tara hung back, almost apologetically. She was about to say something when Vanessa called to her and she ran off.

Charley and George looked at each other incredulously.

'What if Vanessa's the one behind the crimes?' said Charley seriously. George reopened the case file as Charley continued. 'Maybe *she's* stealing the pieces of art and making it look like we did it.'

'Vanessa can't just fly around the world and steal art,' George said. 'At least we know Sam was in both cities at the right time . . .'

'Maybe Vanessa couldn't, but her dad could,' said Charley.

'How?'

'He's a pilot!' Charley hissed. 'I found out when we were in Rome. I was gonna tell you but we got distracted chasing each other in the middle of the night, and I totally forgot until now. Vanessa's dad could easily do her dirty work for her.'

'Like stealing priceless pieces of art from two of the world's most famous museums, then planting evidence to make it look like we did it?' George said.

'Maybe they're doing it together,' said Charley. 'It's just as plausible as the idea of the two of us doing it. In fact, he's got more to gain. Or at least Vanessa does.'

'You really think she would do all that just to be the star of the school again?' George said in disbelief.

'Or to stop us finding out she's stealing songs from around the world.'

George resorted to logic. 'But how did she get one of our flyers? And how would she know the exact pieces of art to steal to make us look guilty?'

'Good points,' agreed Charley. 'But if Vanessa *isn't* the culprit, how does she know we're in trouble again?'

'I might know the answer to that one,' George admitted. 'Someone commented about it on your Insta post this morning.'

'Who?'

'Loredana23,' said George.

'The red-haired girl at the Colosseum!' said Charley. 'The one who came to my show!'

'That's Loredana23?' asked George.

'I don't know. But it could be!' said Charley. 'Maybe Loredana means "red-haired art thief" in Italian.'

'I think that's a bit of a stretch,' said George.

'Either way,' said Charley, 'she was definitely acting suspiciously.'

George looked dubious.

'Write it down,' urged Charley. 'We can't discount anyone.'

George started typing again.

'How much did this Loredana know about the theft?' asked Charley.

'Not much. They just said something had been

stolen. Didn't say what.'

'So how did Vanessa know about the erased emperor?'

George looked up from his typing. 'That's a good question. Maybe she *was* in Rome after all.'

'I've got an idea,' said Charley, spying Principal Haverstock across the schoolyard. 'Come with me.'

Charley strutted towards the head teacher, who was nervously fiddling with her lanyard while gazing at the top of the main school building.

'Do you think a loose roof tile could kill a child?' Principal Haverstock asked absent-mindedly.

'Ummm, I – I'm not sure,' answered Charley.

'The inspectors seem to think so,' continued the principal, almost to herself.

Charley coughed nervously as George followed the principal's gaze.

'Did I hear you say you were looking at student records recently?' asked Charley, trying to sound as innocent as possible.

'Hmm? Oh yes, I spent all Monday going over them with the inspectors,' Principal Haverstock replied.

'We were just wondering who had the best attendance record out of Tara and Vanessa,' said Charley.

George could see what she was doing and admired her creativity. It was exactly the type of skill he'd known she would bring to the investigation.

Principal Haverstock was still distracted by the roofing conundrum. 'Definitely Vanessa. That girl hasn't missed a day all year.'

Charley looked crestfallen. Vanessa couldn't have stolen the art herself if she was at school. Still, that didn't let her father off the hook.

'Are you all right?' The principal finally focused on her students.

'We're fine,' said Charley casually.

'I'm worried about you two,' said Principal Haverstock. 'I'm going to suggest your parents get together and consider whether this tour should continue.'

'Wh-what?' stuttered Charley. 'Why?'

'I'm not sure all this carry-on is good for your health,' the principal explained gently. 'Especially after what happened in Rome.'

The bell rang and Principal Haverstock jumped. 'Off to class!' she ordered before striding off.

'Why does she have to get our parents involved?' asked George.

'We just have to hope they'll let us keep touring,'

said Charley, looking for the bright side.

'You know what else we need to hope for?' said George. 'That Sam doesn't tell Officer Neilsen he left the apartment in the middle of the night. If he does, there's no chance we'll be able to continue the tour.'

CHARLEY AND GEORGE'S CASE FILE

SUSPECT 1: Sam Mullane

Why do we suspect him?

Not in his room the morning the theft in Amsterdam was discovered.

Looked and smelled like he'd been out all night.

Lied about his key card.

Recently came into money.

Definitely left the apartment in Rome during the night.

What's his motive?

Money?

How did he do it?

Might have worked with a staff member from the Colosseum?

SUSPECT 2: Vanessa Devine

Why do we suspect her?

Knows a lot about the thefts.

What's her motive?

Jealous of Charley's fame and wants to make Charley look bad?

Doesn't want us finding out she's stealing songs.

How did she do it?

Her dad is a pilot. Maybe he's stealing the art for her?

SUSPECT 3: Red-haired girl

Why do we suspect her?

She was at the Colosseum and at the show in Rome, and she ran away both times.

Could she be Loredana23?

What's her motive?

???

How did she do it?

???

DAY 9 – *3.45 p.m.*
Goddard Road, LONDON

Charley sat in her kitchen and tried to imagine the type of music that would accompany the scene before her. Something domestic and yet ominous at the same time.

Seated at the small wooden kitchen table were Charley, George, Sam, Charley's mum and George's dad, who was, as you'd imagine, a lot like George: funny, caring and generous. George's mum worked full-time, and his dad liked to refer to himself as the BSAHDE – best stay-at-home dad ever.

'Personally I think the tour should continue,' said Sam. 'We've invested too much to call it off now.'

Interesting that Sam's first concern is money, thought Charley. In fact, it seemed to be his only concern.

'However,' Sam continued, 'your principal thought we should have a meeting in light of . . . current circumstances. So the floor is open.'

George's dad spoke first. 'Thank you, Your Honour.' He winked at George. 'I think Principal Haverstock was right to call us together. I know it was Miss Fairburn's decision to let Charley and George go on tour, but a principal needs to look out for the well-being of her students too. And so do we.'

'Oh, I'm your student now?' joked George.

'Yes,' deadpanned his father. 'At the school of life.'

Charley smiled.

'Which is why I think we should consider pausing the tour.'

Charley's smile disappeared. As did George's.

'Not forever,' said George's dad quickly. 'Just until this whole . . . business is over.'

No one seemed to want to actually mention the crimes in front of them.

'I'm sorry,' George's dad continued, 'but your mental health is more important than your careers. I just want you two to be happy.'

There was a beat, then Charley's mum spoke.

'Well, I think they should keep touring. Charley and George have both worked very hard to get where they are, and there's no way either of them would do something illegal. Why should their success be ruined by someone else's stupidity?' She looked as though she was addressing a courtroom. Charley imagined the music shifting from ominous to triumphant. 'These two children are smarter and better people than most adults I know, and they shouldn't be punished because someone else happens to be greedy and selfish and . . . well, an idiot!'

Charley wondered if her mum was going to cry. She also thought she saw Sam shifting uncomfortably in his seat at that last sentence, although she couldn't be sure.

Charley's mum looked to George's dad. 'You're right,' she said. 'We do need to think of Charley and George's well-being. But I think making them sit at home because of someone else's crimes would be worse for their mental health than doing what they love. Besides, you can't take the London show away from them. Charley's been looking forward to it for weeks. And so have I.' Charley's mum held her hand over her heart. 'I really want to see my daughter perform live.' She locked eyes with Charley. 'You shouldn't let anybody get in the way of your dreams.'

Charley's eyes welled with tears.

'Excuse me,' said Charley's mum, standing up and walking hurriedly from the room.

'Well, that was dramatic,' said George, reusing Principal Haverstock's line.

'And emotional,' added Sam, looking uncomfortable.

'And brilliant,' finished Charley, beaming.

'I might go and check she's OK.' George's dad stood up and followed Charley's mum out.

'Well,' started Sam, 'I guess . . . the tour is still on?'

'That depends on what Officer Neilsen has to say,' said Charley pointedly.

'Oh, I've already spoken to him,' said Sam. 'We're fine.'

'What did you tell him?' asked George.

'The truth,' said Sam.

'Which is?'

Sam looked slightly confused. 'Which is,' he said slowly,

'that you two can't be involved with the . . . trouble, because we were together the whole time.'

'The *whole* time?' pushed Charley.

'Yes.' Sam's eyes darted between George and Charley.

'What about when you left the apartment in the middle of the night?' Charley asked bluntly.

Sam looked like he wanted to say a dozen different words but couldn't decide which one. 'Wha–? How? I . . .'

'I heard you leave the apartment at one in the morning,' said George quietly, making sure no one outside the room could hear.

'What?' cried Sam. 'I went downstairs for some fresh air. I stood on the street outside the building for a bit.'

Charley and George glanced at each other. Should they admit they left the apartment too, or let Sam's lie stand?

Charley spoke first. 'Then why weren't you anywhere to be seen when we went after you?'

'You left the apartment in the middle of the night?' whispered Sam.

'Only because you did,' replied George.

'Why did you follow me?' Then Sam realized the answer to his own question. 'Do you think *I'm* stealing the art?'

Charley and George didn't know what to say. It's one thing to suspect someone of a crime, but it's another to accuse them to their face.

'Listen,' said Sam. 'I've got just as much to lose as you two. I don't want this tour to end, and I promise you I would never do anything to put it in jeopardy.'

'So where did you go?' asked George.

'I just . . .' Sam seemed to be searching for something. 'I just went for a late-night walk. Spending all day looking after you both can be kinda full on, and sometimes I just need to get out and clear my head.'

'Is that what you were doing in Amsterdam too?' asked George.

Sam looked momentarily stunned, before saying carefully, 'Yes. That's what I was doing in Amsterdam.'

'If Officer Neilsen finds out you left us alone . . . he said he'll shut down the tour,' warned Charley. 'And if he doesn't, our parents will.'

'Well then we'd better make sure we stick to the same story,' said Sam. 'That we all spent the entire night in the apartment.'

Charley and George fell silent. To keep touring, they'd have to go along with Sam's lie. Or at least not expose the truth. They weighed up what to do next: tell the truth and have the tour shut down? Or stay quiet, keep doing shows and try to solve the crimes themselves?

'Is everything OK?' asked Charley's mum, re-entering the room with George's dad.

'Yes, everything's fine,' answered Charley stiffly.

But it clearly wasn't.

DAY 9 – 4.30 p.m.
Priory Park, LONDON

George and Charley sat opposite each other in the park, holding milkshakes.

'So now what?' Charley was so overwhelmed by the day's events that she hadn't even begun to drink her vanilla malt. Her brain was so rammed with information it had forgotten how to drink a milkshake, and maybe even what a milkshake was.

'Well, I don't think we can count on Officer Neilsen to get to the bottom of this,' said George. He had devoured his chocolate shake so quickly it seemed his brain had decided they were in the World

Shake-drinking Championships.

'Not if his only suspects are the two people we know for sure are innocent,' said Charley. 'Do you think Sam is telling the truth about his late-night walks?'

'Not for a second,' said George. 'He's definitely lying about something, but I don't know what.'

'And what about Vanessa?' asked Charley.

'What about her?'

'We know she wasn't in Rome on Monday, but we need to find out if her dad was.'

'Hmm.' George lobbed his empty cup perfectly into the bin. 'Maybe it's time we snoop.'

'We what?' asked Charley.

'We do what all good detectives do,' replied George calmly. 'We snoop.'

'Snoop?'

'Yep.'

'Where?'

'Around.'

'What are you talking about?' said Charley, amused.

'Every criminal case in the world has been solved by someone having a good old snoop around. No one ever snoops anywhere specific.' George launched into a potential comedy routine. 'You never hear an investigator say, "I'm gonna have a snoop under the sofa" or "You snoop downtown, I'll snoop uptown." They always just snoop . . . around.'

George's improv gave Charley an idea. 'I know what we can do.' She reached for her phone. When she found the site she was looking for, she scrolled for a phone number then gave the phone to George.

'No!' he protested.

'You can do it,' she said calmly.

'How?'

'Do what you do best,' she replied. 'Improvise.'

Charley was the one believing in George this time. Her faith was just what he needed. His heart thumping, George thought for a moment, took a deep breath, tapped the number and waited.

'Hello, British Airways customer service, Deanna speaking. How may I help you?'

'Hello? Hello?' said George in a voice he hoped sounded like a doddery old man.

'Hello,' came the response.

'Can you hear me?' said George, refining his character's voice.

'Yes, I can hear you.'

'What's your name?' asked George.

'Deanna,' came the shouted reply.

'Diana?'

'No, Deanna.'

'Oh,' said George. 'Nice to meet you, Diana.'

'It's – oh, never mind,' she said, frustrated. 'How can I help you?'

'I wanted to say thank you to one of your pilots,' said George.

'I see . . .'

'Yes,' continued George. 'I was coming back from Rome yesterday, where I was visiting my granddaughter, er . . . Sharon. She's got a job there working as a nanny while she studies Italian.'

'Uh-huh.' Deanna sounded slightly bored.

'Anyway, I had a lot of bags with me on my way home. I like a bit of Italian fashion, you know, the odd Armani, the occasional Versace.'

Deanna chuckled.

'Well, I was trying to find the check-in when I dropped one of my shopping bags, and one of your nice pilots picked it up and chased after me. Lovely man, he was, and I just wanted to send a message thanking him for his help.'

Deanna sighed. 'I'll see what I can do. Do you remember his name?'

'Well,' said George, going in for the kill, 'that's where I hoped you could help me. Unfortunately my memory isn't what it was, and I can't quite remember the surname.' He paused for effect, then continued, 'I think it started with a D though.'

'I may need more than that.' Deanna laughed.

'Yes, of course, Diana,' said George, eliciting another chuckle. 'It was a fancy name, I think. Debonair. Or Dilettante. Or Devine. Something like that. I don't suppose you could check for me, could you?'

There was silence as Deanna mulled over the request. George hoped against hope that his old-man voice, combined with his comedy timing, might just convince her.

'What's your name, please?' she asked.

For a brief moment, George panicked. Should he give his own name or someone else's? His own name might come back to haunt him, but the wrong name could arouse suspicion.

George took a punt. 'My name's Gerald. But you can call me Gerry.' More silence. And then . . .

'Stay on the phone for me, please, Gerald. I mean, Gerry. I'll see what I can do.'

Bingo!

The hold music began to play, and George looked to his partner for a thumbs up. Unfortunately Charley could only hear one side of the conversation and had no idea whether or not it was going well. She turned her palms upward instead, the universal sign for 'What's going on?'

George put the phone on speaker, so she could listen too.

For a moment, the music provided a soundtrack to the park, then Deanna returned. 'Are you there, Gerry?'

'Yes, I'm here,' answered George.

'One of our pilots, Captain Devine, was in Rome yesterday. He must have been the person who helped you.'

Charley punched the air. George was so shocked that he almost forgot to be Gerald. Almost.

'Well, then,' said George. 'Could you please pass on a message to Captain Devine, saying that Gerry wants to thank him for finding his bag and returning it?'

'I would love to,' said Deanna with a smile in her voice.

'Thank you so much, Deanna,' said George, saying her name correctly as an extra treat. 'You've been incredibly helpful.'

'It was my pleasure,' she replied. 'I hope you have a lovely day, Gerry.'

'Oh, I will now,' George said brightly. 'Goodbye.'

He tapped the screen to make sure the call had ended, then looked up at Charley.

'That. Was. Amazing,' said Charley.

George returned Charley's phone. He was suddenly hit by a combination of nerves, terror and the aftermath of drinking a milkshake too fast. 'I think I'm going to be sick.'

But Charley was excited. 'So Vanessa's dad *was* in Rome when the plate was stolen!' she said triumphantly. 'She has just gone to the top of the list of suspects. I think we need to interrogate Vanessa. And, if she doesn't tell us the truth, we'll threaten to tell everyone that her songs are stolen.'

George wondered if Charley might be enjoying this a little too much. 'Great,' he replied weakly. 'But can we do it tomorrow? I think I might need to go home and have a lie down.'

'Of course,' said Charley, suddenly noticing George didn't look well. 'But, first, take this.' She held out her milkshake with both hands.

'Why?' asked George.

'It's an Oscar for Best Performance,' said Charley.

'I'm touched,' said George, clutching the shake/ trophy in one hand and putting the other hand to his heart. 'I haven't prepared a speech. I'd like to thank my agent for her support, my best friend, Charley, for believing in me, and most of all I'd like to thank Gerry for being my inspiration. I love you, Gerry, wherever you are.'

As they made to leave the park, Charley's eyes flitted from a child in a blue football jersey practising his skills to a grey-haired woman chasing a dog that had escaped its lead. There was a group of older kids from Rokesbourne High listening to music, and a man attending to a crying baby in a pram. And there, half hidden by a tree, was a girl in her twenties, with a nose piercing and a shock of red hair.

'Don't look now, but I think we're being followed,' said Charley.

'Let me guess,' said George. 'Red hair and nose piercing?'

'Spot on. First she was at the Colosseum, then the show, and now here.'

'But why is she following us?' asked George.

'There's only one way to find out. We need to talk to her!'

'As soon as we approach her, she'll run.'

'I know,' said Charley, trying to look like she was still having a normal conversation with her friend, and not plotting to sneak up on the person watching her have the conversation. 'That's why you need to leave the park by the side gate, go round to the bottom entrance and sneak up behind her.'

'Why me?'

'Because I'm the one she's following. If I leave the park, she'll follow me. As long as I stay here, she won't move. But leave slowly,' Charley directed. 'And don't look at her. Otherwise she'll know we're up to something.'

Charley held up her hand for a high five, like she was saying goodbye. George tossed Charley the milkshake Oscar, which bounced off her open palm and on to the ground, where it exploded in a milky mess.

'Why did you throw a milkshake at me?' Charley gasped.

'I thought you were asking for it back! Why did you hold your hand up?' said George.

'For a high five! I thought it would look natural!'

At the same time they remembered why they

had been trying to look natural in the first place and instinctively turned their heads to see if their audience of one suspected anything. The red-haired nose-pierced onlooker clearly hadn't – until the two people she was spying on looked directly at her.

She ran.

Charley shouted, 'Go!'

George's wheels spun.

This time the chase really *was* on.

★

Accelerating from a standing start is really tough in a wheelchair, but once George got up to speed he was on a roll. Literally.

He was adept at steering his chair round obstacles, but he'd never had to do it at such a pace before. He rocketed across the basketball courts, pushing forward with one hand and backwards with the other to dodge scooters, rollerbladers and, of course, basketballers.

Approaching the side entrance of the park, George had two choices: slow down and carefully manoeuvre his way out of the gate, then turn left on to the footpath and try to build up speed again; or maintain his pace, stick his left hand out, grab the gate post and slingshot himself round it.

He went with the more time-efficient option,

marvelling at how something could be quite so scary and enjoyable at the same time. Ahead was a steep downhill path of about a hundred metres, leading to a roundabout, but it was dotted with people. George couldn't guarantee his own safety or that of the people in his way, so he made a split-second decision – to veer out on to the road.

He wasn't sure if it was luck or excellent timing that saw him zoom seamlessly through the gap between two cars. Probably a little bit of both. He let the hill take care of his speed, which was rapidly increasing, and focused on steering himself away from any potential collisions. The drivers didn't know whether to honk their horns or give way to the kid in the wheelchair threatening to overtake them.

The roundabout at the bottom of the hill loomed. George needed to make a sharp left turn when he got there, and head along Priory Road before re-entering the park through the bottom gate – but this time there was no gate post to hold on to. George half-checked, half-hoped that there was no approaching traffic, pulled the sleeve of his jumper over his left hand and slammed it down on the wheel.

The metallic rim tore through George's sleeve but

the resistance was enough to slow the rotation of the left tyre. The right wheel continued to spin, turning the wheelchair to the left. It was a move George had only pulled off in a hallway before, and never at this velocity.

People gasped and stared as they watched George zoom smoothly into the corner. Coming out of the roundabout, however, the laws of physics took hold and the wheelchair started to tip. Everything seemed to move in slow motion as George's right wheel stayed clamped to the ground, while the left one, well, left. George tried to calculate the maximum angle he could hit before he lost the ability to right himself, and figured it was about forty-five degrees.

As the chair hit forty-three, George thought, *I may have misjudged this.*

DAY 9 – *4.48 p.m.*
Priory Park, LONDON

George arrived at the gate at the bottom of the park with a skid and a look of absolute horror on his face. Like he'd just seen a ghost – his own.

By his calculations, his chair had reached an angle of around forty-seven degrees, but a combination of a well-timed gust of wind, some skilful balancing and the weight of the unused flyers in his backpack had righted him. Blocking the exit from the park, he hoped the red-haired girl with the nose-piercing wouldn't have the athleticism to leap over him.

She didn't.

Turning back, the potential suspect saw Charley a few metres behind her and realized she couldn't get away. With a resigned droop of her shoulders, she submitted to her fate and stood panting between Charley and George.

Charley wasn't quite panting, but she was certainly puffing. George was outright wheezing.

A moment passed as all three tried to catch their breath. Charley bent over, hands on her hips, George stared straight up at the sky, and the girl crouched down on the grass beside the path.

Charley tried to speak first, but every word was punctuated by a breath. 'Why – *puff, puff* – are – *puff, puff* – you – *puff, puff* – following – *puff, puff* – us?'

'It's not – *pant, pant* – what it – *pant, pant* – looks like.'

'Explain – *puff, puff* – yourself – *puff, puff* – then!'

'I think – *pant, pant* – I might need to sit down – *pant, pant* – if that's OK.'

'OK.' Charley was slowly regaining her breath. 'But don't run away again.'

'I don't think I could,' the girl joked, rolling backwards from her crouch into what could only be described as a sprawl.

George looked and sounded like he was trying to throw up a harmonica, so Charley decided to lead the questioning. 'Who are you and why are you following us?'

'My name's Ruby Sherring, and I'm a journalist,' replied the young woman. 'Well, I *want* to be a journalist. Actually, I eventually want to be a *scriptwriter*, but for now I want to be a journalist.' She picked at a blade of grass. 'I work at *M*. You know, the music magazine?'

Charley and George were not only aware of it; they dreamed of being in it.

Internally, Charley cried, *OhMyGodI'veAlwaysWanted ToBeInThatMagazineEverSinceIStartedPlayingMusic PleaseCanWeBeBestFriends?*

Externally, she said, 'I've heard of it.'

'I'm an intern, which basically means I make coffee

for everyone,' said Ruby. 'I thought if I could write a good story about Europe's newest music sensation, maybe they'd give me a proper job as a writer.'

'Why didn't you just ask Charley for an interview?' said George, finally able to speak again.

'I was going to,' said Ruby. 'But I wanted to see you in action first, so I paid for my own ticket to Rome. I had time to spare during the day so I decided to visit the Colosseum. It was a complete fluke that you were there as well. When you saw me I kinda panicked and ran.'

'What about at the show?' Charley was still sceptical.

'When you spotted me again, I was afraid you'd think I was a creepy stalker, so I ran out.'

'So . . . to prove you're not a creepy stalker, you followed us to a park and spied on us from a distance?'

'I'm sorry,' said Ruby, blushing. 'If it helps, I didn't just spy on you in the park. I watched you at school as well.'

'That doesn't help at all,' said George.

'You're right. It actually sounds worse,' Ruby groaned. 'I'm really sorry! I just wanted to get a sense of what your lives were like before I sat down and talked to you. I had a whole article planned out, about how artists are using social media to bypass big record companies and take their music to the world. I wanted to interview you both about how someone with real talent can succeed without a huge publicity team backing them. Or maybe they succeed *because* there isn't a huge team behind them. Now I've completely messed the whole thing up.'

Ruby lay back on the grass, defeated.

Charley examined the girl in front of her and decided that she was telling the truth.

'Well . . . not completely. We're working on something pretty big at the moment.' She shot George a glance. 'We can't tell you what it is, but, when it's done, how about we give you the exclusive story?'

George frowned at Charley and opened his mouth, but she gave him a look that said, *Hold on for a second*.

'Really?' Ruby beamed, sitting back up. 'You'd do that for me?'

'What do you think, George?' asked Charley with a raised eyebrow.

'Sure,' George replied, although he had to admit he wasn't at all sure what was going on. However, he too was taken in by Ruby the budding writer, partly because she'd said she wanted to interview him as well.

'Oh my goodness,' Ruby gushed. 'How exciting!'

'Although – ' Charley hesitated – 'it might be best not to mention it to anyone at the magazine just yet.'

'Of course,' said Ruby, pretending to zip her lips shut.

'So . . . what's it like working at *M Magazine* anyway?' Charley couldn't help herself.

'Oh wow, look at the time,' said Ruby, glancing at her phone. 'I really should be getting back to the office. I told them I was going out to get coffees two hours ago.'

In one swift movement, Ruby hopped to her feet, collected her backpack and was off.

'I'll ping you my deets on Insta,' she shouted as she left.

One question was still bugging George. 'So what's this big thing we're working on at the moment?'

'The art thefts,' said Charley. 'Don't you think the whole thing would make a brilliant story?'

'Sure,' George said drily. 'As long as it doesn't end with us in jail.'

Charley's face dropped. At no point had she even considered that Ruby's article might have an unhappy ending, let alone one that saw them imprisoned. Did twelve-year-olds go to prison? Even if they didn't, everyone at school would read Ruby's article and then they'd all think Charley was a thief. Oh, this could be a disaster!

Charley didn't say any of this out loud, but George could read it all on her face.

'So is Ruby still a suspect?' he asked gently.

'I don't think so,' replied Charley. 'I trust her. But that means we still don't know who Loredana23 is.'

'It's been a big day,' said George, 'and it's getting dark. Let's go home and get some rest. There's still plenty to do if we're gonna catch the art thief.'

Charley sighed.

'Don't worry,' he added. 'I have no doubt it will all work out.'

In truth, though, George had plenty of doubts.

CHARLEY AND GEORGE'S CASE FILE

SUSPECT 1: Sam Mullane

Why do we suspect him?

Not in his room the morning the theft in Amsterdam was discovered.

Looked and smelled like he'd been out all night.

Lied about his key card.

Recently came into money.

Definitely left the apartment in Rome during the night. When confronted, said he was out walking.

Lied to Officer Neilsen about where he was.

What's his motive?

Money?

How did he do it?

Might have worked with a staff member from the Colosseum?

SUSPECT 2: Vanessa Devine

Why do we suspect her?

Knows a lot about the thefts.

What's her motive?

Jealous of Charley's fame and wants to make Charley look bad?

Doesn't want us finding out she's stealing songs.

How did she do it?

Her dad is a pilot, and he was in Rome when the theft happened.

SUSPECT 3: Loredana23

Why do we suspect her?

Suspicious comments on Instagram. (We know that Ruby isn't Loredana23.)

What's her motive?

???

How did she do it?

???

DAY 10 – *1.00 p.m.*

Rokesbourne High School, LONDON

Charley and George had intended to use their lunch break to revise the case but they were collared by Miss Fairburn.

'I was hoping I could have a quick chat with you in my classroom,' she said, chasing them down the hallway.

They made their way back to Miss Fairburn's room, and she swung the door open. This action was immediately followed by all three of them saying a word that shouldn't be repeated in polite company.

Put simply, the door fell off.

The one good hinge could no longer take the strain of a job meant for two, and the door clattered to the floor with a thud. Next came a tinkling sound as the cracked glass in the door gave up the fight and shattered.

It was hard to pick who said the most offensive word, but if you had to choose it was probably Miss Fairburn.

There is something very funny about hearing your teacher swear, and Charley and George looked at Miss Fairburn in both horror and amusement.

'I'm so sorry,' she said sheepishly.

'That's OK,' said George. 'So are we.'

Miss Fairburn crouched down and began to carefully pick up the glass. Charley offered to help, but her teacher waved at her to stay back.

'This isn't going to help Principal Haverstock's mood,' muttered Miss Fairburn.

'What do you mean?' asked Charley.

'The inspectors were here again on Tuesday,' admitted Miss Fairburn. 'I managed to distract them from the door, but they said the school was badly in need of repairs. The student records were passable, but only just. Principal Haverstock now has to prove to them that we can find the money to fix the school, as well as maintain the records and improve Rokesbourne's reputation.' Miss Fairburn paused, as if considering whether she should stop talking, then continued at a whisper. 'They're threatening to merge us with Queenswood High, which means Principal Haverstock could lose her job. They'll only keep the school open if they're confident it meets certain standards.'

'Is one of those standards that all doors must be attached to door frames?' asked George.

'I would imagine so,' replied Miss Fairburn, smiling wryly.

'So what did you want to talk to us about?' asked Charley.

Miss Fairburn began to answer, but she was interrupted by the arrival of Principal Haverstock, who had heard the commotion. 'My door!' the principal cried, followed a little too slowly by, 'Is everyone all right?'

'We're fine,' said George. 'Miss Fairburn was about to tell us something important.'

Miss Fairburn looked stunned. 'I – um – yes – well,' she spluttered. 'I brought the children here to give them their next assignment.'

'Oh good,' said Principal Haverstock. 'I'm dying to hear what you've come up with.'

'Right now?' asked Miss Fairburn.

'No time like the present,' said the principal.

'Oh, OK then.' Miss Fairburn scurried into the classroom to find her notes.

She soon returned to Charley, George and Principal Haverstock, still gathered round the fallen door. 'Your next show is in the French city of Tours, next Thursday.'

George remembered the look on Sam's face when he announced that one of the places they'd visit on tour was called Tours. Sam seemed to think it was the best joke he'd ever made. In many ways, it probably was.

'Sam suggested you go a day early to explore the surrounding area, and I think that's a wonderful idea.'

George thought he could hear Principal Haverstock's teeth grinding.

'Leonardo da Vinci once lived in a chateau nearby, and I think it's the perfect place to visit.' Miss Fairburn's pride in her research was evident in her voice. 'According to the website, the chateau has a variety of da Vinci's mechanical inventions. However, I want you to pay close attention to the painting of the *Mona Lisa*. It's not the original, but I want you to take note of its story. How it came to be there and, in particular, why it's so famous.'

'The *Mona Lisa*, eh?' said Principal Haverstock thoughtfully. 'I look forward to reading your report on that.'

'Ah yes, the reports,' said Miss Fairburn. 'I haven't received one since Copenhagen.'

'We're sorry,' said George. 'It's just that with everything that's been going on –'

'It's OK,' said Miss Fairburn. 'You can hand them all in at the end of the tour.'

Did Principal Haverstock just grind her teeth again or was that a shard of glass under her shoe? George wondered.

'Well!' the principal announced suddenly. 'This door needs more than just gaffer tape. I'll go and fetch the caretaker. If we still have one . . .'

Once Principal Haverstock was out of earshot, Miss Fairburn spoke again. 'I heard about what happened in Rome and I am so sorry. I can't believe that the exact piece of art I told you to study was stolen *again*. I mean, what are the chances?' She let out a nervous laugh.

Charley and George gave her weak smiles.

'Anyway, I'm sure this trip will be much less eventful.' Miss Fairburn returned to the task of picking up pieces of glass and wood.

'I certainly hope so,' said George.

Charley's attention was drawn to something inside the classroom. Her expression changed, she furrowed her brow, and she turned to face her teacher. 'How's your mother, Miss Fairburn?'

'She's, um, she's fine, thank you.' Miss Fairburn sounded rather flustered.

'Did you manage to find a care home for her?' Charley asked.

'Oh yes. Yes, I did.'

'That's so good to hear,' said Charley. 'You must have worked very hard to pull the money together.'

'Thank you, Charley. Yes, I did. Although it's not quite there yet. I still need one more thing to fall into place.' Miss Fairburn's cheeks suddenly flushed. 'Anyway,' she blurted, 'as long as you two are OK, that's all I care about.'

'Oh, don't worry about us. We'll be fine,' said Charley coolly. She swung her backpack over her shoulder, nodded to George that it was time for them to leave and set off down the hallway.

George smiled at Miss Fairburn then followed Charley. 'What was that about?' he asked when they reached the schoolyard.

'The flyer!'

'What flyer?'

'The flyer we gave Miss Fairburn,' Charley hissed under her breath. 'The one she pinned above her desk. It's gone.'

'So?'

'Maybe that's the flyer that turned up in Rome.'

George thought it over. 'You think *Miss Fairburn* stole the art?'

'She said she found a care home for her mother, but last week she told us how expensive they were. Then she said she needs one more thing to fall into place.' Charley paused for effect. 'Like maybe selling a valuable piece of art!'

'Are you sure the flyer's missing?' George asked, a little hesitantly.

'Well, it certainly wasn't on the wall,' said Charley.

'Maybe it fell off. Did you look on the floor?'

'If you don't believe me, go back and look for yourself.'

'I believe you,' said George. 'But I might go back and check the floor. You never know. Perhaps it's under her desk.'

George wheeled back to the classroom, trying to think of an excuse for why he had returned.

The door was still in pieces on the ground, so George poked his head round the gap where the doorway used to be. Miss Fairburn had her back to him, her phone to her ear.

'If all goes well, I'll have the money by the end of the month. In fact, if all goes well, we won't have to worry about the money ever again.' She paused. 'No, the children don't suspect. Although I do need to tread carefully – Charley was acting a little strangely just now.' Another pause. 'I know. I need to stay in their good books. Without Charley and George, the plan falls apart. And no plan means no money.'

George's mind raced.

'Anyway, I'd better go,' said Miss Fairburn. 'I shouldn't really be talking about this here.'

George spun his wheels to turn and, as he did, they made a tiny squealing sound. Did Miss Fairburn hear? He didn't dare hang around to find out. In that moment, the flyer was forgotten.

★

Back in the schoolyard, Charley sat open-mouthed as George described what he had heard. She didn't know whether to feel shocked or smug, so settled on a bit of both.

'So I guess we add Miss Fairburn to the list of suspects,' George said reluctantly.

'I think we have to,' said Charley. 'She's the one who's been telling us which famous pieces we're supposed to visit and study – and those are the pieces of art that have always gone missing afterwards. If it's just a coincidence, it's a pretty big one! Plus she's the only other person who had a flyer, and that flyer is missing. *And* we know she can now afford to put her mother in a nursing home.'

'But how could she have stolen the art?' countered George.

'She must be working with someone else,' said Charley. 'Miss Fairburn could be telling them what to steal, then helping them make it look like we did it – by giving them a flyer that no one else has, for example.'

'I really don't want to suspect her,' said George.

'Neither do I,' said Charley, 'but she's acting

suspiciously. We don't have a choice.'

George nodded.

'I hate to say it, but write it down.'

George grabbed his iPad and added the new information to their growing case file.

'Now,' Charley said, with a flicker in her eyes, 'let's have a chat to Vanessa. But let's keep what we know about her stolen song up our sleeve until we need it.'

★

'Oh, look – it's the terrible two,' said Vanessa haughtily as they approached.

'Can we ask you something?' Charley said calmly.

'Sure.' Vanessa looked around at the assembled Deviners. 'Is it about how to do a show without being called to the principal's office the next day?'

The Deviners smirked. Charley held her nerve.

'Perhaps you need some advice on international law?'

The Deviners giggled. Charley stayed steady.

'Or maybe,' said Vanessa, her tone serious, 'you'd like to know what to do when your fans turn against you.'

The Deviners folded their arms. Charley started to crack.

Sensing Charley's unease, Vanessa turned the knife. 'I've seen what they're saying about you on Instagram,' she sneered. 'I wonder what will happen when they find out you're a mean little thief.'

Charley snapped. She could handle the personal insults but no one messed with her fans. 'You're the thief!' she shouted.

'Me?' said Vanessa innocently.

'You've been stealing songs and claiming them as your own!'

This was not the plan, thought George.

'That's not true!'

'Really?' said Charley. 'So is it just a coincidence that there's a song in Italy that sounds exactly like yours?'

Vanessa looked offended, shocked and humiliated all at the same time. 'I don't know what you're talking about,' she said.

Charley half-sang, half-taunted, '*Mambo Salentino*.'

Vanessa took two steps towards Charley and somehow managed to whisper-shout, 'How dare you? I write every one of my own songs, and for you to suggest otherwise is simply t-t–' Vanessa stuttered – 'treasonous! How do you know *they* didn't steal *my* tune?'

George suppressed a laugh, but Vanessa spotted it.

She came closer to Charley, until their noses almost

touched, and hissed, 'I can end your career in a second.'

'Really?' said Charley. 'And just how would you do that?'

'I have my ways,' answered Vanessa. 'Maybe I've already started.'

CHARLEY AND GEORGE'S CASE FILE

SUSPECT 1: Sam Mullane

Why do we suspect him?

Not in his room the morning the theft in Amsterdam was discovered.

Looked and smelled like he'd been out all night.

Lied about his key card.

Recently came into money.

Definitely left the apartment in Rome during the night. When confronted, said he was out walking.

Lied to Officer Neilsen about where he was.

What's his motive?

Money?

How did he do it?

Might have worked with a staff member from the Colosseum?

SUSPECT 2: Vanessa Devine

Why do we suspect her?

Knows a lot about the thefts.

SAID SHE HAD ALREADY STARTED TO RUIN CHARLEY'S CAREER!!!

What's her motive?

Jealous of Charley's fame and wants to make Charley look bad?

Didn't want us to find out she's stealing songs.

How did she do it?

Her dad is a pilot, and we know he was in Rome when the Colosseum Museum theft happened.

SUSPECT 3: Loredana23

Why do we suspect her?

Suspicious comments on Instagram. (We know that Ruby isn't Loredana23.)

What's her motive?

???

How did she do it?

???

SUSPECT 4: Miss Fairburn

Why do we suspect her?

Every piece of art that's been stolen has been the same art she's told us to go and look at. This feels like too much of a coincidence!

The flyer we gave her is missing and there was a

flyer found in Rome.

What's her motive?

Money so she can afford a nursing home for her mother.

How did she do it?

Working with someone else?

DAY 10 – 3.45 p.m.
Caryn Street, LONDON

Charley had barely spoken since the showdown with Vanessa in the schoolyard. Not only had she lost her temper *and* the argument, she had blurted out the one thing they were saving as leverage against Vanessa.

After school George thought a change of scenery was called for, so he suggested going to his house. They found his dad in the front garden, digging out some stubborn weeds.

'Here they are, the two partners in crime!' he said cheerily.

The look on George's face said it all.

'Sorry,' he said. 'I just meant, you know . . .'

'It's OK,' said Charley. She flashed George's dad a weak smile, and she and George made their way into the house, where Charley sat limply on the couch.

George did his best to lift her spirits. 'Why do they call it a sitting room? It's not like we have a standing room or a lying-down room.'

Charley's mouth curled up at the edges slightly, showing the tiniest bit of appreciation for George's joke.

'Listen,' began George softly, carefully, 'we're gonna be OK.'

Charley nodded, almost imperceptibly, while staring at her feet.

'And you know how I know we're gonna be OK?' said George.

Charley shook her head, once again barely moving.

'Because we're innocent,' said George calmly. 'We're not going to be convicted of anything, because we haven't done anything. No matter what happens, we've got the truth on our side. This whole thing is like one giant maths problem. No matter how hard the equation looks, there *is* an answer. We just need to find it.'

Charley scrunched up her face at the very mention

of maths. 'I don't even know where to start. The more work we do, the more confusing it becomes. We've now got four suspects, all of whom look as suspicious as each other. And we still don't know who Loredana23 is. They haven't even posted any photos on Instagram. Just comments after my videos.'

'I know,' said George, trying to sound soothing.

'Sam keeps going out on his own in the middle of the night, Vanessa knows as much about the crimes as we do, and Miss Fairburn's flyer might have been the one that was found in Rome,' said Charley in a rush. 'Meanwhile Vanessa's dad was in Rome on the night of the theft, Sam has come into some money, and so has Miss Fairburn.'

'It *is* a lot to take in,' said George.

At that moment, the door to the sitting room creaked open and George's dad entered, carrying a tray with two cups of hot chocolate, two biscuits and two marshmallows. He placed the tray down carefully and slipped out again.

Charley reached forward and picked up a single marshmallow, then placed it carefully atop her hot chocolate. George thought it looked like a tiny pink lifebuoy.

'So what do we do now?' asked Charley tentatively.

'We need a new plan. Our investigating is good, but we need to do something different. Something creative.' George looked to Charley, hoping to spark her interest. 'We need to do something inventive in Tours.'

'I'm not sure I can do it,' whispered Charley.

'The investigating or the show?' asked George.

'Both.' Charley sighed. 'I don't have the energy. Maybe we should just cancel the tour, admit defeat and end my career.'

Silence descended as Charley's words sank in. George wanted to plead with Charley to do the show, to remind her that tickets had already been sold and that she'd be letting down all her fans if she cancelled.

'But you haven't done anything wrong!' he began, then stopped, realizing that the last thing Charley needed today was another argument. He could see the anxiety and exhaustion in his friend's face. He sighed. 'If you choose not to do the show, I'll be right behind you.'

Charley's shoulders relaxed slightly, as if a weight had been lifted off them.

George decided it was time to change tack. 'Let's write a song!'

'About what?' Charley looked uncertain.

'I came up with a title,' said George, opening the

notes app on his iPad. 'Aha! "Smells Like Home".'

'Sounds more like a comedy routine to me.' Charley chuckled, her mood slowly lifting.

'Fine then,' said George. 'If you won't write it, I'll do it myself!'

A small smirk started to appear on Charley's face.

'You can keep your hotels, with your fancy key-card locks. All I wanna wake up to is a pair of stinky socks.'

The smirk became a smile.

'I don't need a window with a lovely ocean breeze. I just need my mum's fridge, full of stinky cheese.'

The smile turned into a grin, so George delivered the final blow.

'No more will I travel, to Amsterdam or Rome. When my dad farts in the hallway, it smells like home!'

'I heard that,' yelled George's dad from the kitchen.

Charley and George properly laughed then, and for a moment all their worries disappeared.

'Come on then,' said Charley. 'If we're gonna do it, we may as well do it properly.'

George watched with relief as Charley reached into her backpack and pulled out her notebook. The colour came back to her cheeks.

'I've got it!' she exclaimed suddenly.

'Told you it was a good song title,' said George

smugly.

'No,' said Charley. She had forgotten all about the song. 'I know how we can catch the thief in Tours.'

'How?'

'We set a trap.'

'I'm listening,' said George.

'We stake out the chateau,' said Charley. 'If the thief is stealing the things Miss Fairburn tells us to study, then the *Mona Lisa* will be the next target.'

'But what about the show?'

'The show's the next night,' replied Charley. 'Remember? We're flying over a day early. Which means we've got a night off to keep an eye on the *Mona Lisa*.'

'OK,' said George. 'But Sam will notice if we take off on our own. And we certainly can't stay out all night.'

'No,' said Charley triumphantly. 'But Ruby can!'

'That may be the best idea you've ever had.'

'Thank you.' Charley reached for her phone. 'I'll call her now.'

George watched as his best friend and co-detective opened her Instagram messages, found Ruby's number, rang it and put the phone to her ear. After a few seconds, she mouthed 'voicemail' then began her message. 'Ruby, it's Charley. Call me back. Immediately. Byeeee!'

Charley was fidgety now, and her feet were tapping the floor. 'I'll try her at work,' she said, opening up her browser and typing in '*M Magazine*'.

Charley tapped the screen again, then put the phone to her ear and waited. Again.

'Hello, I'd like to speak to Ruby Sherring, please.'

A pause.

'Ruby Sherring. She's an intern.'

Another pause.

'Are you sure?'

A long pause.

'OK then, my mistake.' Charley hung up.

'What?' asked George.

'There's no one who works there named Ruby Sherring.'

Charley's phone pinged in her hand. It was a message from Ruby.

Sorry. Was on a work call. Meet you in the park in 30?

Charley showed George the message.

'Well,' said George, 'this should be interesting.'

Charley and George watched with keen eyes as Ruby approached them.

'So.' Ruby breezily dropped her backpack to the ground, then flopped down next to it. 'What's so important?'

Charley got straight to the point. 'You don't work at *M Magazine*, do you?'

'Yes, I do. I'm an intern,' said Ruby.

'We just rang them and they've never heard of you,' said Charley.

Ruby exhaled like a tired horse.

'OK, I lied about working at *M Magazine*,' she admitted. 'I do *want* to work there though, and I *am* writing an article to submit to them. But no, they don't know who I am.'

Charley and George stayed silent, unimpressed.

'I'm sorry,' said Ruby. 'I thought you'd be more open to being interviewed by me if I was connected to *M*, even if I was only an intern.'

'How do we know you're not lying now?' asked George.

'I'll show you.' Ruby reached into her backpack and

pulled out a laptop. She opened it, hit a few keys then turned it to face Charley and George. 'Here's what I've written so far.'

A document with the title 'Charley P and George C' was on the screen. George felt a slight tingle at seeing his own name in the headline. He read the first few paragraphs, then lifted his head.

'You're a really good writer,' he said. 'And you've clearly put a lot of work into this.'

Ruby sighed. 'They'll probably edit it down.'

Charley and George were conflicted. On the one hand, they really wanted to trust the girl who said she would put them in the pages of their favourite music magazine, but, on the other, she had lied about working at that magazine. On a third hand, she had actually written a really great article about them.

George decided that three hands were better than one. He nodded ever so slightly to Charley. She nodded back.

'All right, we believe you,' said Charley. 'But no

more lies.'

'I promise,' said Ruby, raising her hand as if to take an oath. 'No more lies.'

'Good.' Charley relaxed.

'Wait, is that why you wanted to meet me?'

Charley and George exchanged glances again, then Charley spoke. 'No. We need you to help us solve some crimes.'

'So there *are* crimes!' Ruby blushed as she realized who she was speaking to. 'I saw your comments on Instagram,' she explained. 'I don't know who Loredana23 is, but they do not like you.'

Charley and George took turns filling Ruby in on exactly what had happened: the stolen painting in Amsterdam and the key card left behind, the plate in Rome and the incriminating flyer. They listed the suspects: Sam, his new phone and his dodgy night-time walks; Vanessa, her jealousy, and her dad's trip to Rome; Miss Fairburn, her missing flyer and her mum's care home; and the mysterious Loredana23.

Finally they told Ruby their plan to stake out the chateau.

She looked excited, then scared, and then excited again. 'This would make for an amazing article,' she realized.

'The show in Tours is next Thursday,' said George. 'One week from today. So we need you at the chateau the night before.'

'Yay! We can all travel over together.'

'No,' said Charley. 'Sam can't know about the plan – or about you. You'll have to make your own way there.'

'Hmm. I guess I could borrow my mum's car. How far is it to Tours anyway?' Ruby checked her phone. 'Eight hours? Well, I guess if I left London first thing, I could be there when the chateau closes. Then I could stay in my car for the night and keep an eye out for anything – or anyone – suspicious.' She did some calculations in her head. 'Can I still come to the show?'

'Sure.' Charley smiled.

'All right then.' Ruby extended her hand. 'Let's do it.'

Charley shook Ruby's hand then looked at George. He placed his hand on top of theirs.

The investigation was back on.

'The tour's coming to Tours'

57,402 views

Top comments

MiaCucina OMG. There actually was a theft on the same night as Charley's Roma show.

At the Colosseum. It was on the news.

> **Loredana23** Told you so.

MarlouVR @Loredana23 was right about the robbery at the Van Gogh Museum too.

> **Loredana23** Yep.

LeilaToomler I don't feel right sleeping in her shirt any more.

> **Loredana23** I'm not sure Charley is the person we thought she was.

MonstresorJude Don't know if I want to go see her in Tours. What if she steals my wallet?

> **Loredana23** Hahahahaha
> **MayZee** You're all losers.

PART 3

TOURS

VIP GUEST

Château du Clos Lucé, FRANCE

Charley Parker was living her best life. The November sun warmed her cheeks as she strolled through the lush gardens of the Château du Clos Lucé.

This was a very good idea, she thought.

The gardens were clearly well-tended, but in a way that looked natural. A placid stream wound its way through the trees, traversed occasionally by old wooden bridges. But not just *any* old wooden bridges – bridges designed by Leonardo da Vinci himself.

There was a swing bridge that could be pulled back to the bank whenever a boat needed to pass. There was also a double-decker bridge that could take a horse and cart on the lower level and pedestrians on the upper deck.

In a small clearing sat an enormous wooden tortoise shell that looked like a cross between a wine barrel and a UFO, but was actually the world's first military tank. Downstream there was a paddle wheel, alongside another wheel that somehow allowed a six-year-old to lift a slab of stone five times their own weight with pulleys and levers.

And every one of these objects was invented by Leonardo da Vinci.

If you had asked Charley who Leonardo da Vinci was before today, she would have said he was a painter, maybe a sculptor. Meandering past some of the most influential inventions in human history, Charley felt bad that she hadn't known the full extent of da Vinci's genius. It was like only knowing Paul McCartney for that song he made with Rihanna, then discovering he was also in the Beatles.

The gardens were still, calm, tranquil – and they made Charley feel the same way. On any other day, she probably would have felt a bit stressed to be wandering alone through the scene of a potential future crime, of which she knew she would be the main suspect. Today, though, she felt relaxed, because she knew Ruby was on her way. Sometimes all you need is a good plan.

Charley turned back towards the entrance to the chateau, where she caught sight of Sam deep in conversation with a tour guide.

Flirting again, thought Charley.

'Flirting again,' said George.

Charley jumped and emitted a tiny shriek.

'Sorry,' said George. 'I didn't mean to scare you.'

'And I didn't mean to make the sound of a squirrel slipping on ice,' said Charley.

Sam looked towards them slightly sheepishly, then ended his conversation and walked over.

'Shall we start the tour?' He brandished three tickets.

There were a dozen or so tourists in the gardens, but only Charley, George and Sam made their way to the door of the chateau. An official-looking guide with an official-looking pass hanging round her neck led the trio inside, into the most magnificent bedroom Charley had ever seen. It looked like the set of a medieval movie, except this was real life. A majestic four-poster bed stood in the middle, with drapes hanging from every corner.

'This is where Leonardo da Vinci lived,' said their

guide, Celeste. The three small flags under the name on her pass indicated that she spoke French, English and Italian. 'The great inventor slept in this very room.' She paused dramatically. 'And died here too.'

'Awkward,' said Charley under her breath.

'Da Vinci was of course born in Italy, but he was invited to the chateau by the king of France in 1516. Leonardo crossed the Alps on a donkey, carrying his precious notebooks and three paintings that he didn't want to leave behind. Do you know what those paintings were?' Celeste asked.

When no one answered, she continued, '*The Virgin and Child with Saint Anne, Saint John the Baptist* and the most famous one of all – the *Mona Lisa*.'

Charley's heart skipped a beat.

'Take your time to look around the room,' said Celeste. 'Then we will move on to the study.'

George was off like a rocket-powered rollerblade, but Charley wanted to stay for a bit. She tried to imagine the greatest inventor of all time, Leonardo da Vinci, sleeping in this actual bed. Gazing out of that window. Sitting on that chair. She could almost picture him in her mind, could almost see him in the room.

Charley peered down to the foot of the bed and spied a small metal pot. She decided it was best not to imagine what da Vinci did in that.

She followed the others to da Vinci's study. Against the wall was a wooden bookshelf full of curios: seashells,

animal skulls, eggs, an hourglass, a starfish and a preserved bat, sitting among so many other things.

On the other side of the room, an ornately carved chair faced a desk with an open book on it, and a quill and ink. Hovering over the desk were two shelves of books that looked as though they had been stolen directly from Hogwarts. Charley glanced around the room again to see if anyone suspicious caught her eye but, aside from Celeste, it was only Charley, George and Sam there.

A table by the window was strewn with notebooks. Charley studied them intently. Was this Leonardo da Vinci's actual handwriting? She peered at the strokes of the letters, the beautiful way the end of the feather's spine had created words on a page. Once again she imagined the great inventor himself scribbling away.

Next they entered the dining hall, and there on the wall hung the painting they had come to see: the *Mona Lisa*.

Charley peered into the eyes of the woman in the painting. She gazed back at Charley with a slightly bemused expression. Was she smirking? Was she smiling? Was she frowning? Charley couldn't tell, but she found herself drawn in. Then, aware of what had happened the last time she'd stared at a painting for too long, Charley backed away.

She was startled by Celeste's voice in her ear. 'Don't worry. It's not the actual painting. The real one is in the Louvre Museum in Paris.'

Charley nodded as if she hadn't already been told that by Miss Fairburn. She wondered if Celeste knew about the previous thefts.

'This copy is still quite precious though,' Celeste continued. 'It is thought to have been made a hundred years after da Vinci died, by the man who was painter to the queen of France.'

A thought popped into Charley's head, and she turned to look out through the ground-floor window and into the courtyard. She spied a bench that would be a perfect vantage point for Ruby to keep an eye on the painting, at least until the chateau closed.

Charley relaxed a little at the possibility they may soon solve the crimes. She floated through the rest of the rooms like a happy ghost. There was a kitchen full of fruit and vegetables, with dried food hanging from the ceiling; another room adorned with beautiful faded tapestries; and finally a modern room containing an exhibition of yet more of da Vinci's creations.

There were model boats, model cars and parachutes – even a model of the first-ever helicopter – all accompanied by da Vinci's own sketches. Charley was entranced. She reminded herself to thank Miss Fairburn for finding this place when they went back to school.

'I hope you have found today interesting,' said Celeste.

'Thank you, I did,' said Charley. 'Very much.'

'I like your badge, by the way,' said Celeste.

Ah yes, thought Charley. *The badge.*

Vanessa had approached Charley and George in

the schoolyard the day before they left for Tours. She was carrying what she called 'a peace offering'.

Vanessa had used her time in Mr Brown's art class to create Rokesbourne High School badges with the slogan *senza pensieri*. (According to Vanessa, this was a Latin phrase meaning 'with a sense of thought'.) Vanessa insisted that Charley and George wear the badges on tour and give them out to fans as a way of promoting the school.

Principal Haverstock overheard the words 'promoting' and 'school' and thought the badges were a wonderful idea. 'Anything to enhance the school's reputation,' she'd said, taking a badge for herself.

Charley had intended to remove her badge the second they left England but she'd forgotten, which is why it was now being commented upon by their tour guide.

'Thank you,' said Charley. 'It was a gift.'

'It is very amusing,' said Celeste.

'Thank you,' Charley said again, although she wasn't sure what was so amusing about it. She looked around for George, thinking she could fish an extra badge from his backpack and present it to the friendly guide, but he was nowhere to be seen.

'Here, you can have it.' Charley unpinned the

badge. 'I've got plenty at home.'

'Oh, *merci beaucoup*!' Celeste said. 'That is very kind of you.'

Charley left the chateau and ambled back outside into the cool Loire Valley sunshine. In the gardens the autumn leaves were beginning to fall, the ducks were dozily drifting and marvels of science were dotted around the grounds. Charley hadn't felt so peaceful and content since before the first theft in Amsterdam.

'Shall we have something sweet?' asked Sam, noticing the crêperie in the courtyard.

'Absolutely,' replied Charley.

Best. Day. Ever.

Charley, George and Sam found a table just in time to see Ruby enter the grounds of the chateau. Ruby immediately spotted them, but pretended not to.

While Sam was distracted with the menu, Charley nodded her head towards the room that contained the *Mona Lisa*, then used her eyes to indicate the bench where Ruby could begin her stakeout. Ruby clearly had no idea what Charley was doing, but, after thirty seconds of more nodding, some eyebrow raising and eventually pointing, the message was received and understood. Ruby took a seat on the bench. The plan was in action.

1   Keep an eye on the *Mona Lisa* until closing time to see if anyone tries to remove it.

2   Once the chateau grounds close, watch from the car to see if anyone leaves with the painting.

3   Check the *Mona Lisa* is still there when the chateau opens in the morning.

4   Message Charley and George if anything suspicious happens.

Charley and George devoured their crêpes gleefully – George ate his with the classic lemon and sugar, while Charley had chocolate, banana and caramel. As always, George was stunned by her capacity for sweet-eating.

Later, as they left the crêperie, there were brief winks between them and Ruby. In fact, they all tried so hard not to look like they were working together that the three of them nearly ruined it by bursting into laughter.

Charley could feel a tingle of excitement in the air and she knew George could feel it too. Either nothing would happen tonight and they could happily do a show without being accused of another theft, or something would happen and they'd have caught a criminal.

It was a win–win situation.

★

DAY 16 – 7.30 p.m.
The Old Mill House, Villeloin-Coulangé, FRANCE

'Guys, I'm really sorry but I have to go back into Tours for a bit,' said Sam. 'I know our rule, but I desperately need to go through a few things with the venue owner. You kids will be all right here on your own for a little while, yeah?'

'Of course,' replied George cheerily. 'We'll be fine. Take as long as you need.'

George had been helping Charley put the finishing touches on the lyrics of 'Smells Like Home'. They were in the kitchen of the house Sam had found for them near Tours.

In any other circumstances, Charley and George would have been shocked at Sam's suggestion, but they raised their eyebrows knowingly at each other as he collected his jacket and car keys. Was Sam really going to meet the venue owner, or was he actually heading back to the chateau? Either way, they knew that Ruby was in place and, if Sam did anything wrong, she'd be there to witness it.

The door closed, the car started, and Sam drove away.

Charley found herself secretly hoping he *was* about to steal the painting, just so the case would finally be closed. She didn't admit that though.

'Is it really bad that I kind of hope he's about to steal the painting?' said George. 'Just so the case is finally closed. That's bad, isn't it?'

Charley grinned to herself. 'I still think "Smells Like Home" would be better as a comedy routine,' she said, returning to the song.

'I dunno,' said George. 'I'm not sure it's all that funny.'

'Ooh!' Charley remembered her exchange with Celeste at the chateau. 'It might be worth looking up the phrase on Vanessa's badges. The tour guide today seemed to find it amusing, but I'm not sure why.'

George opened up his iPad and searched '*senza pensieri*'. Then he started laughing.

'What?' Charley said.

'So Vanessa was half right. *Pensieri* does indeed mean "thoughts".' George waited a moment. 'But *senza* does not mean "sense".' He paused again. '*Senza* means . . . "without". Which means that Vanessa's badges actually say, "Rokesbourne High School . . . Thoughtless".'

Charley burst out laughing. 'Do you think she knew that? And gave us those badges on purpose? Or was she actually trying to be nice?'

George was frowning at something on his screen. 'Wait a minute . . .'

He flipped the iPad round to show Charley. One of the search results was a song called 'Senza Pensieri'. George clicked on the link and a dance beat kicked in, accompanied by Italian lyrics.

'Unbelievable!' cried Charley. 'She's stolen another song!'

But George didn't join in. He stared at the screen as if he had seen the monster in a horror film before anyone else.

'What?' asked Charley.

'Look at the singer,' said George.

Charley read the name on the screen out loud. 'Fabio Rovazzi.'

'Keep reading,' urged George.

'Featuring Loredana Bertè.' Charley looked at George.

'Loredana!' George repeated.

There was only one conclusion, and they reached it at the same time.

'Loredana23 is Vanessa Devine!'

DAY 17 – 9.07 a.m.

The Old Mill House, Villeloin-Coulangé, FRANCE

Charley woke up in an armchair with a crick in her neck. She and George had attempted to stay up for the entire night in case Ruby spied anything suspicious at the chateau and, to be fair, they had almost made it. They had relied on a combination of excitement, nerves and jelly babies to stay awake. Charley even considered making a coffee until she remembered how bad Sam's espresso had smelled.

Charley figured she must have fallen asleep around 4 a.m. and she knew for sure that Sam hadn't returned home by then. Opening her eyes now, she focused on

George, who was directly opposite her. While Charley was lying partly on her side in the armchair with her head at a weird angle, George had passed out in his wheelchair, his head tilting almost ninety degrees backwards.

Charley couldn't work out how he could breathe, let alone sleep.

Ruby had kept them updated with regular messages throughout the night, although there had been very little to report.

5 p.m.
Chateau closing. Mona Lisa still in place.

6.15 p.m.
Staff leaving. Nothing suspicious.

7.45 p.m.
Still nothing.

8.28 p.m.
Bored now.

10.23 p.m.
Think I just saw a bat. Might have been an owl.

10.26 p.m.
Are there even bats in France?

10.28 p.m.
Just googled it, and yes there are.

10.31 p.m.
Can bats break into cars?

The messages had continued until 3.35 a.m., but there had been nothing since. Had Ruby fallen asleep as well?

Charley stared at her phone, willing it to display a new message. With a buzz and a tinkle, it did exactly that. For a second Charley wondered if she had somehow developed special powers.

With a snort and a grumphle, George sat bolt

upright. 'What does it say?' He showed no signs of discomfort after his gravity-defying sleep.

Charley took a deep breath, surveyed the screen and read aloud: '*Chateau open.* Mona Lisa *still there, same weird smile. No crime committed!*'

Charley and George stared at each other.

'I don't know if I'm relieved that nothing was stolen or disappointed that we didn't catch the thief,' said Charley.

'I feel the same.' George rubbed his neck. 'Someone could still steal the painting tonight though.'

'True.' said Charley. 'But both thefts happened right after we visited the museums. And those museums were in walking distance of where we were staying. The chateau is a half-hour drive away.'

'I think we're off the hook,' said George, nodding slowly. 'Maybe now we can just enjoy the show, and the rest of the tour.'

Hearing George's words, Charley's shoulders dropped. Then her whole body relaxed. She hadn't realized just how tense she was. Even at the chateau she'd jumped when George had come up behind her. Now, as the stress left her body, she remembered what it felt like to be normal. Well, as normal as a twelve-year-old rockstar accused of two art thefts could feel.

George was right – they could kick back and enjoy the rest of the tour, without wondering if there was going to be another crime.

Charley looked down at her phone and tried to find an emoji that reflected her emotions. Was there one that was simultaneously happy, relieved and conflicted? Instead she wrote:

> Thanks for the update. Try to get some sleep. See you at the show.

'So now what?' asked George.

'We do what we came here for.' Charley beamed. 'Do a show, have fun and work on a new song.'

'But what about Vanessa? And Miss Fairburn? And Sam?' said George. 'We don't even know if he came home last night.'

Charley held a finger to her lips and George stopped talking. They waited a second, then another second, then a third second. Eventually a familiar cartoon snore came from Sam's room.

'OK,' said George. 'Sam made it home, but we still don't know what he's been up to.'

'We can worry about that when we get back to London.' Charley's eyelids were starting to droop. 'For now, let's just get some rest.'

Charley and George went to their respective rooms, where they did their best to make up for the lack of sleep. At first Charley just looked at the ceiling with a smile on her face, certain that, although the string of art crimes had not been solved, she and George were at least partly off the hook. When she did eventually drift off, it was the best sleep she'd had in ages.

★

DAY 17 – 3.05 p.m.
Maximus nightclub, TOURS

Charley and George had arrived at the venue for Charley's Tours show feeling both excited and relieved, and they were now slouched on the couches of Charley's dressing room.

In truth, the word 'dressing' made the room sound a lot fancier than it actually was. After the 500-seat theatres and concert halls Sam had booked up until now, this venue could only be described as dingy.

They were yet to see the actual stage, but if the backstage area was anything to go by, they weren't in for much. The carpet was frayed and strangely sticky, the walls were covered with the scribbled names of bands that had previously played there and the only mirror in the room was as cracked as Miss Fairburn's door. The whole place left Charley wondering why Sam had chosen this as a tour venue.

Two voices travelled down the corridor, first at a murmur, then a mumble, rousing Charley and George from their couch-slouches. They tried to identify the speakers. The first voice was clearly Sam's but the other also sounded vaguely familiar. Formal. Official.

'What's *he* doing here?' asked George curtly as he spied the owner of the voice through the doorway. Charley followed George's gaze and saw Officer Neilsen standing in the corridor, still deep in conversation with Sam. 'Maybe he's come to tell us that nothing was taken from the chateau and that we're clearly innocent, then grovel on his hands and knees for our forgiveness.'

She grinned.

'I hope so.' George imagined the scenario and found he enjoyed it.

Sam led the police officer into the dressing room, where he immediately took a seat, carefully smoothing his trouser legs.

'There's been another theft,' said the officer abruptly, instantly ending George's daydream.

'What?!' exclaimed Charley. 'Where?'

'At the museum you visited yesterday,' answered Officer Neilsen, checking his notepad. 'The Château du Clos Lucé.'

'But how?' Charley sounded almost helpless. 'It was there this morning . . .'

'What was there this morning?' asked the officer.

'The *Mona Lisa*!' shouted Charley. 'The painting we were told to study!'

'That's not what was stolen,' said Officer Neilsen calmly, scribbling in his notepad.

'What *was* taken?' asked George.

Officer Neilsen flicked back a few pages and read from his own handwritten notes. 'The stolen item was a priceless small notebook that once belonged to Leonardo da Vinci.'

Charley's blood ran cold. Not only had there been

another theft, but once again the stolen item happened to be something Charley had spent a lot of time looking at.

'This was found at the scene.' The officer held up one of Vanessa's badges in a plastic bag.

While George sat forward in his seat, Sam shifted uncomfortably in his.

Charley sighed in defeat. 'Of course it was.'

'You recognize this then?' asked Officer Neilsen.

'Yes,' admitted George. 'I had a heap of them in my backpack.'

'And where are they now?' said the officer.

'I thought they were all still there,' said George.

'Except . . .' Charley hesitated. 'I gave mine to the tour guide.'

'I see.' Officer Neilsen started scribbling again. 'That's convenient.'

'Someone's setting us up!' Charley was stung by what he was implying.

The officer seemed to consider this possibility, then without looking up from his notepad he asked, 'And have you been with the children the whole time in France?'

'Who, me?' asked Sam, startled, before realizing there was no one else in the room that question could have been directed at. 'Yes, I've been with Charley and George at all times,' he lied.

Charley didn't know whether she should say anything. Was it a crime to sit by in silence while someone lied to a police officer? If she spoke up, would she incriminate Sam? She glanced at George, who shook his head almost imperceptibly.

Officer Neilsen stood up, walked across the room, examined his reflection in the cracked mirror, then turned to face them. 'Three crimes in three countries, all at museums you visited, and all with evidence linking you to the crimes.' He let the significance of that sentence settle in before he continued. 'For the life of me I can't work out why two twelve-year-olds with the world at their feet would want to get mixed up in something like this.'

'Are they still going to be able to do the show tonight?' Sam had a worried look on his face.

'The show should be the least of your concerns,' replied the officer. 'I'm considering taking Charley and George into custody here and now.'

Silence filled the room like an overinflating balloon. Everyone knew what was happening, but no one wanted to make it burst.

George took it upon himself to pop it. 'Listen,' he

said, 'we're on the verge of cracking this case. If you can give us until Monday, I guarantee we'll have found the culprit.'

Officer Neilsen seemed amused. He was impressed by George's confidence and intrigued by the proposal.

'Oh, *you're* on the verge of cracking the case, are you?' he said in the same slightly patronizing tone he had used the first time they'd met him. 'Well, I suppose I should just step aside and let the professionals take over.'

Charley didn't appreciate his sarcasm.

'Please,' George added for good measure.

The inspector took a deep breath in, then exhaled. 'It's against my better judgement, but all right. However, if you don't have the culprit by Monday, I'll have to arrest you both.'

The word 'arrest' made George imagine a whole bunch of other words, including 'guilty', 'handcuffs' and 'prison'.

'So can they still do the show or not?' Sam piped up. George thought he seemed strangely oblivious to the mood in the room.

'Yes,' replied the officer warily. 'They can still do the show.'

'Would you like to stay and watch?' asked Sam.

'Thank you, but no,' said the officer, checking his watch. 'If I leave now, I might just make it back to Amsterdam before my daughter goes to bed.'

'OK then.' Sam clapped his hands together as if nothing had happened. 'Let's do a show!'

For the first time in Charley's life, performing was the last thing she wanted to do.

DAY 17 – 5.15 p.m.
Maximus nightclub, TOURS

Charley was shattered. Her life had been a roller-coaster ride these last few weeks, and now she just wanted to get off. The highs were exhilarating, but the lows were devastating. She was desperate for something in the middle.

She watched listlessly as George brought Ruby up to speed with the latest developments. 'Run me through what you saw,' he said when he'd finished.

'Absolutely nothing,' said Ruby. 'I spent the afternoon with my eyes glued to the *Mona Lisa* and no one came near it. When the chateau closed, I went back to my car and watched from a distance. I saw half a dozen tour guides leave at around six o'clock, then nothing for the rest of the night. Apart from a creepy bat.'

'What about the notebooks? Did you see anyone take one of them?'

Ruby racked her brain. 'I mean, when I was sitting on the bench I might've seen a tour guide come over and rearrange them,' she replied uncertainly. 'But I couldn't be sure.'

'Is it possible the tour guide actually took one of them away?'

'I – I guess so,' said Ruby hesitantly.

'And could you identify that guide if you had to?'

'Not really.' Ruby shrugged. 'I'm sorry. I was so focused on the *Mona Lisa* that I didn't really pay attention to anything else.'

'What about when the tour guides left the chateau?' pushed George. 'Did any of them look suspicious?'

'No. I studied each of them carefully, but no one was carrying a painting.'

'What about a notebook?'

'I don't know,' said Ruby. 'I wasn't looking for a notebook!'

'Oh, this is hopeless!' cried Charley suddenly. 'Why

don't we just admit we're beaten? Someone is clearly trying to set us up and they're obviously smarter than us. We tried to catch them, but they still stole something. No matter what we do, we just can't win. Let's just give up and admit that two twelve-year-olds can't solve a string of international art thefts.'

George and Ruby glanced at each other.

George tried to sound encouraging. 'Charley, I just think if we all put our heads together we can still work this out.'

'We did put our heads together,' Charley snapped, 'and it got us nowhere!' She stood up, uncertain of where to go next, but knowing she didn't want to stay where she was. 'If you'll excuse me – ' her voice cracked – 'I'm going to prepare for my farewell show.'

And, with that, Charley Parker left the room.

★

DAY 17 – 6.45 p.m.
Maximus nightclub, TOURS

George was sitting in his normal position behind the camera, filming Charley as she sang on stage. But this was hardly a normal show.

For starters, Maximus was not Charley's normal kind of venue. The 'stage' was really a raised dance floor with a railing round it, meaning there was barely enough room for Charley's band. They were standing so close to each other that they kept bumping elbows. There was barely enough room for Charley.

At least they'd solved one mystery: they now knew why Sam had chosen this place. The owner, Max, who'd named the club after himself, was an old friend of Sam's.

'Sam, *mon ami*,' Max had boomed an hour earlier when he'd arrived backstage. 'How long has it been? Two, three years?'

Before Sam could answer, Max had turned to Charley and George. 'Your manager is a good man, but always trying to make money.'

George had glanced at Charley, but she hadn't returned his look.

'Shame you're such a terrible card player,' Max had said to Sam. 'But after tonight we're even, no?'

Sam had put his arm round Max and hustled him out of the room, saying, 'Let's talk about this outside,' but it was too late. They were obviously doing the show here because Sam owed Max money.

George pointed his camera at the crowd, but already knew he wouldn't be using the footage. The audience was a mix of regular visitors to the nightclub

(Max had convinced them to buy tickets) and some of Charley's fans and their parents. The regulars looked uncomfortable about watching a twelve-year-old sing and dance on stage, and Charley's fans looked out of place.

And it wasn't just the audience. There was something missing in Charley's performance tonight: joy. Charley normally exuded happiness from every pore, smiling and beaming her way through each song. Not tonight. When she sang 'Heart Thief', it was clear her own heart wasn't in it.

George knew that promising Officer Neilsen a culprit by Monday was a crazy thing to have suggested, but he had been trying to buy them some time. At least this way Charley could still do the show. But at the moment it looked like Charley didn't even want to do that.

'OK, I've got a new song for you,' announced Charley, her voice empty of all enthusiasm.

The crowd stirred. George refocused the camera, zooming in on Charley.

'It's called "Smells Like Home".'

Some people in the audience chuckled, but not in a good way. The plan was to film the song's debut, put a small clip of the chorus on social media and let the fans take it viral. But, the second Charley began to sing, George knew it wasn't going to be a hit. Charley had come up with a great melody but the lyrics were too jokey. Charley was right – it would have made a better comedy routine.

The song finished. While the audience weren't exactly silent, they were by no means ecstatic. The response could best be described as muted.

George peered at the camera screen and zoomed in tighter on Charley's face. As she smiled politely and thanked the crowd for their applause, George spotted a single tear fall from her eye.

★

Charley knew that the only way to get through the rest of the show was to paint on a fake smile and try not to let the cracks show. That one tear was enough, but no more. Charley decided to simply shut off her emotions and become a robot. A singing, smiling robot.

Ever the professional, she closed the show – and possibly the tour – by thanking the members of her band by name, as well as Sam ('the reason I'm here') and George ('my friend who's always by my side'). As the audience applauded, George couldn't help but think the descriptions of him and Sam could be interpreted negatively. Sam was indeed the reason Charley was here in a grotty nightclub in Tours, and she didn't seem happy about it. And George was always by her side, but right now he wasn't sure if Charley wanted him to be. When Charley said George's name, she turned to smile at him, but it was a polite smile, nothing more. A stage smile.

Turning back to the crowd, Charley said, 'I don't know when I'm gonna get to do this again, so thank you, and goodnight!' Then she launched into an encore of 'Heart Thief'.

Although the audience had already heard Charley sing her hit song once, they lapped it up again (as they did every night). What she may have lacked in heart, Charley made up for in energy. That final song turned the show from a limp five out of ten into a strong seven, maybe even seven and a half. It was by no means one of her best shows, but she did enough to keep her fans happy.

George watched in awe, and a little bit of fear, as Charley smiled her fake smile to the crowd. She stayed on stage a few seconds longer than usual, as if she was taking one last look before giving a final bow and heading towards the dank dressing room.

When Charley passed George, she managed to smile, wave at the crowd, and hiss 'Don't you dare put any of that online' all at the same time.

George had seen Happy Charley, Sad Charley, Angry Charley and Quiet Charley, but this was something else. This was Emotionless Charley.

And she was scary.

DAY 19 – 10.05 a.m.
Caryn Street, LONDON

George didn't know what to do. Charley was like a computer that had gone into safe mode, shutting down all but the most basic functions. She'd interacted with her fans after the show with politeness, but nothing more. She'd responded to his attempts at conversation with short answers, but nothing more. She'd smiled at his jokes on the long drive back to London, but nothing more.

When Sam had dropped George home, George had turned towards Charley hopefully. 'See you tomorrow?' he half-asked, half-pleaded.

'Sure, maybe,' Charley had answered with that polite smile.

'OK,' said George. 'I'll message you.'

As the car had driven off, George had felt like he'd been punched in the stomach with an oversized fist that'd gone straight through and out the other side, leaving air rushing through the hole where his stomach used to be.

Now he was trying to calculate when was best to text. If he waited too long, they'd run out of time to solve the thefts. If he texted too early, Charley might not be fully awake and could find the text annoying. At the very least he needed to wait until she'd eaten breakfast. George knew well enough what Charley was like before she ate breakfast.

At around 10.30 a.m., George finally sent a message. As usual, he wrote descriptions of emojis rather than actually using them. It always made Charley laugh.

> Hope you slept well (snoring emoji).
> Do you wanna meet up and crack this
> case (suitcase emoji)? Let me know
> (let-me-know emoji).

George waited. And waited. He knew the message had been received, but there was no response.

Had he tried too hard? Surely by asking whether Charley wanted to meet up, he was implying that she should let him know. So why did he write 'Let me know'? And why did he write 'let-me-know emoji'? There's no such thing as a let-me-know emoji! But then that was meant to be the joke. This was awful. He'd never overanalysed a text to Charley like this before.

Eventually George saw three little dots appear. Charley was composing an answer. His heart jumped. His head pounded. His nerves jangled. Then the dots went away.

A second later they started again. Once again George studied those dots, trying to interpret their meaning. And once again they stopped.

George took this to be a good sign. He imagined Charley was trying to compose the perfect response, with a clever retort and some made-up emojis of her own. For a moment George allowed himself to smile, guessing what his friend's response would be. Then it came.

> Nah, you got this. See you Monday.

Wow, thought George. *That's cold.*

The wind whistled through the hole in his stomach once again.

DAY 19 – *11.40 a.m.*

Caryn Street, LONDON

George felt helpless. Hopeless. Charleyless. He tried to recap the case in his bedroom, but it was so much harder without his best friend.

'Who do we suspect?' he asked. There was no response.

George replayed the events of the last few days in his head, wondering if Sam could still be the culprit. Maybe their manager hadn't been flirting with the tour guide at the chateau . . . Maybe he'd been asking her to steal da Vinci's notebook. Perhaps he'd collected it from her later that night, when he'd said he was meeting Max.

George suddenly had a thought. When Max had seen Sam at the venue before the show, he'd said, 'How long has it been? Two, three years?'

That's not a thing you'd say to someone you'd caught up with the previous night: Sam had lied about meeting up with Max!

George was excited but realized that he had no one to share the feeling with. He reached for his iPad and tapped in the extra information.

CHARLEY AND GEORGE'S CASE FILE

SUSPECT 1: Sam Mullane

Why do we suspect him?

Not in his room the morning the theft in Amsterdam was discovered.

Looked and smelled like he'd been out all night.

Lied about his key card.

Recently came into money.

Definitely left the apartment in Rome during the night. When confronted said he was out walking.

Lied to Officer Neilsen about where he was.

Left the Mill House in France the night before the gig and lied about meeting Max.

What's his motive?

Money? Max said Sam was bad with money – did Sam lose money to him playing cards?

How did he do it?

Might have worked with staff members of the museums. He gave his number to Sandra at the Colosseum and was sneakily talking to a guide at the chateau.

George knew this wasn't enough to prove that Sam was guilty, but there was a lot here that was suspicious. And if Sam *was* the culprit, George still had questions. For example, was it just a coincidence that Sam had stolen items that Charley and George had spent time looking at? Was he trying to make it look like Charley and George were the thieves or was he accidentally leaving things connecting them to the thefts – like the flyer and the badge – behind?

George wanted to ask Charley these questions.

Scrolling down, he looked at what they knew about Vanessa, and did a little cut-and-paste to combine it with what they knew about Loredana23.

SUSPECT 2: Vanessa Devine

Why do we suspect her?

Knows a lot about the thefts.

SAID SHE HAS ALREADY STARTED TO RUIN CHARLEY'S CAREER!!!

VANESSA IS LOREDANA23!!! She has been posting about the thefts online and turning Charley's fans against her.

What's her motive?

Jealous of Charley's fame and wants to make Charley look bad.

Didn't want us to find out she's stealing songs.

How did she do it?

Her dad is a pilot, and he was in Rome when the Colosseum Museum theft happened.

Once again, though, there was no piece of concrete evidence that proved Vanessa was guilty. And, if *she* was guilty, what had Sam been getting up to all this time?

Scrolling again, George read the notes they had made on Miss Fairburn.

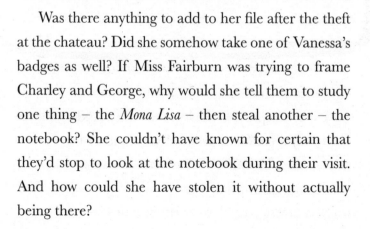

SUSPECT 3: Miss Fairburn

Why do we suspect her?

Every piece of art that's been stolen has been the same art she's told us to go and look at (or was right next to it). This feels like too much of a coincidence! The flyer we gave her is missing and there was a flyer found in Rome.

She can now afford a nursing home for her mother.

What's her motive?

Money so she can afford a nursing home for her mother.

How did she do it?

Working with someone else?

Was there anything to add to her file after the theft at the chateau? Did she somehow take one of Vanessa's badges as well? If Miss Fairburn was trying to frame Charley and George, why would she tell them to study one thing – the *Mona Lisa* – then steal another – the notebook? She couldn't have known for certain that they'd stop to look at the notebook during their visit. And how could she have stolen it without actually being there?

So many questions, no one to ask. George glanced at his phone again and reread the last message Charley had sent him: *Nah, you got this.*

George wasn't sure he'd 'got this' at all.

He was missing something, and it wasn't just Charley. He was searching for the clue, the hint, the one equation that would solve the whole maths problem, but the more George stared at the case file, the less sense it made.

He needed a change of scenery and he knew exactly where to go – Whiskers on Kittens. If he couldn't talk to Charley in person, he could at least go where he would feel her presence.

Unfortunately the journey to the cat cafe made George feel like he was in a music video for a song about lost love. As he made his way through the park, he thought back to the phone call he and Charley had made to British Airways. The violins would've kicked in as he passed Rokesbourne High School, reminiscing about the first time he saw Charley in the schoolyard. And the song would have reached its crescendo as George approached the cat cafe, smiling at the memory of planning the tour with Sam and Charley.

George imagined himself gazing through the window and seeing Charley sitting at their regular table.

Then he shook his head. It was all just a daydream. The music video came to an end and another song began.

Strangely enough, when George actually arrived at the cat cafe, he saw Sam sitting at their usual table. George blinked, wondering why he was daydreaming of Sam and not Charley. He looked again.

Sam was still there.

Was this a hallucination? Or was George actually in a music video? Was Sam his lost love?

Making a snap decision not to go into the cafe, George hid behind some wheelie bins across the road. If Sam was doing anything untoward, this might be George's last chance to catch him in the act.

Sam was deep in conversation with a woman who had her back to the window. She looked familiar but George couldn't quite place her. Was it Sandra, the tour guide from the Colosseum? Or was it one of the guides from the chateau? Why would she have come all the way to London to meet Sam? And, if she was an accomplice to a string of daring art thefts, surely Sam wouldn't be so bold as to meet her in a public place?

Eventually the two stood up to leave. As Sam's lunch partner turned to face the door, George gasped.

It was Miss Fairburn.

Now it was time for the music video to rewind: George raced back home, away from the cat cafe, past school and back through the park. The music was frantic and muddled now, playing in reverse.

George arrived home, panting, and took the iPad from his backpack. He looked at the last note he had made for Miss Fairburn: *Working with someone else?*

Could Sam and Miss Fairburn be in this together? That would certainly explain how Sam knew which pieces of art to steal. And it would explain how Miss Fairburn could be involved in the thefts without leaving school. Had this whole thing been organized by the two of them so that Miss Fairburn could put her mother in an expensive nursing home, Sam could become rich, and Charley and George could be framed as the culprits?

George had so many questions, but only some answers. And, without Charley to bounce ideas off, he was stuck. He felt like fish without chips, ribs without wings, jerk without chicken. George chuckled to himself, remembering that Charley was both vegetarian and addicted to sweet food. He imagined her saying, 'Disgusting!' and himself replying, 'Fine then, how about French toast without maple syrup?'

But Charley wasn't there.

George spent the rest of Saturday and all of Sunday trying to find a clue that hadn't yet been discovered. He made notes, drawings, lists and diagrams. He went over every detail of every trip they had taken, trying to identify anything that might have seemed innocent at the time, but could now be the final key to solving the crime. But nothing came to him.

Most kids go to bed on a Sunday disappointed that they have to go to school the next day. George went to bed knowing that at 9 a.m. he would be meeting Officer Neilsen to supposedly reveal the identity of a criminal mastermind.

★

George awoke on Monday with a knot in his stomach. Actually, multiple knots. Like a scout had been practising tying knots over and over again on the same piece of rope, and then George had swallowed that rope. The knots stayed put as he ate breakfast, dressed for school and tried to crack the case all at once.

As he approached the office of Principal Haverstock, George still had a list of unanswered questions. At the top of that list was this one: Could he, George Carling, solve a string of international art thefts, and save himself and his best friend?

Oh well, thought George as he opened the door. *Now's the time to find out.*

CHARLEY P INSTAGRAM VIDEO

'The Tour's coming to Tours'
59,245 views

Top comments

Mimimimimimi: Why no video from the Tours show? I need my Charley P. xxx

Loredana23 I think we all need to find a new hero. Something was stolen from a chateau near Tours the day before Charley's show. I heard she's the prime suspect – for all three crimes! Along with her friend George!! Party's over, everyone.

> **MonstresorJude** I saw her show in Tours. She was acting strange on stage. Now I know why.
>
> **FlorenceC** I feel sick. I thought she was one of the good ones.
>
> **LeilaToomler** I'm gonna burn my shirt.
>
> **MayZee** I feel like such a loser.

DAY 21 – 9.00 a.m.

Rokesbourne High School, LONDON

'I think we know why we're all here,' began Officer Neilsen officiously.

He was leaning on a bookcase the way detectives do in the movies, being observant while also slightly detached, and George wondered for a moment if the officer might be auditioning for a movie in his own head.

'We're not all here,' said Charley, her eyes fixed to the floor.

George surveyed the room. He and his dad had been the last to enter, and they had found Charley,

Charley's mum, Sam, Miss Fairburn and Officer Neilsen all in place.

He realized then that Principal Haverstock was not behind her desk. In fact, she wasn't even in the room. The hurried click-clack of her shoes in the hallway told everyone she was on her way.

Before now, Charley's mum and George's parents had been assured by Principal Haverstock that there was no need for them to come into the school, that she had everything in hand, and that they would be provided with regular updates. This time, however, they had all agreed that parental attendance was necessary.

The principal arrived in what could only be described as a tizzy. She was flustered and, as was so often the case, she was carrying food.

'Sorry, I didn't have time for breakfast this morning.' She sat at her desk and hurriedly broke apart a croissant, covering her lap and desk in tiny, crusty flakes of pastry.

'Oh, buttocks!' she said, before realizing she was in the company of children and their parents. 'I do apologize,' she added, wiping away the flakes as best she could.

George thought he saw Charley smile a little, but her eyes remained lowered.

'Right then,' Principal Haverstock said. 'I suppose you're all wondering why I called you here.'

There was a pause, then Officer Neilsen resumed control. 'Actually,' he said, 'it was George who called us all here. And we know why.'

Principal Haverstock looked chastened. The officer continued. 'As you know, there has been a series of thefts at the museums the children have visited, on the same days they visited. In every case, the stolen object has been something the children were told to study by Miss Fairburn.'

George coughed quietly but firmly.

'Except in France, where the stolen object was *next to* the piece they were told to study,' the officer corrected.

Did Charley smile again?

'In Amsterdam, a small painting of a pair of boots by Van Gogh was taken. There is a post on Charley's social media featuring the same painting, which Charley has captioned, "*I want!*". A key card from the children's hotel was found nearby, and neither Charley nor George can account for their movements on the morning the theft was discovered.'

Actually, thought George, *we did account for our movements. Those accounts just happened to be different from each other. And Sam's. And Miss Fairburn's.*

'In Rome a plate was taken that featured the emperor Septimius and his family. This time a flyer was found at the scene of the crime – a flyer that no one but Charley or George had.'

And Sam and Miss Fairburn, thought George.

'And in Tours, a priceless notebook once belonging to Leonardo da Vinci went missing. A small badge that could only have been left by either Charley or George was found nearby.'

Or the tour guide Charley gave her badge to, thought George.

'George has promised to reveal the culprit of the crimes today, and I agreed to give him the weekend to prepare his case.' Then Officer Neilsen concluded by speaking directly to George: 'However, if you can't prove your innocence, I'm afraid I will have to take official action.'

George felt Charley flinch beside him. He knew this was his opportunity to save them. He also knew that he hadn't quite cracked the case. He had loads of evidence, but no real proof. Also, he still wasn't sure who to actually accuse.

'George?' asked Principal Haverstock.

This was it. The moment of truth. George was going to have to take a leap of faith. He shifted in his chair, swallowed hard and tried to speak.

'I, um, well . . . Ahem.' This wasn't going well. 'We think . . . Well, I mean, I'm pretty sure the thief is –'

'Vanessa Devine!' Charley blurted out.

★

Charley felt every eyeball in the room spin to look at her, including George's. She hadn't intended to say anything and now, with all the attention on her, she wasn't sure why she had done.

Maybe she'd spoken up to save her friend. Or maybe she'd spoken up because she'd thought George was about to accuse Sam, and she didn't want to see him get in trouble. Perhaps, although Charley would never admit this out loud, she just wanted to get revenge on Vanessa for being so mean.

Either way, it was too late to reconsider. She'd said it and she had to own it.

'Who is Vanessa Devine?' asked Officer Neilsen, confused. 'And why do you think she has been stealing pieces of art?'

'Vanessa is in our class,' said Charley. 'Every time a crime was committed, Vanessa knew about it before anyone else.'

'I see,' said the officer.

'After the theft at the Van Gogh Museum, she said

she wouldn't want to be in our "stolen boots". When we got back from Rome, she said it would be a shame to see "the emperor erased from the painting". Both times she made a reference to the exact item that was stolen. It was almost as if she knew before we did.'

'Hmm.' The officer was thoughtful. 'And what about this time? Did she say anything about the notebook?'

'Not yet,' said Charley. 'But she was the one who gave us the badges we took with us to Tours.'

Officer Neilsen raised an eyebrow.

'Maybe she wanted us to take the badges so she could place one at the scene of the crime and make it look like we did it!'

'But how?' asked Principal Haverstock. 'She hasn't had a day off school all year.'

'No,' Charley said. 'But her dad's a pilot. And we found out that he was in Rome at the same time we were. So maybe he was also in Amsterdam and Tours.' Charley shot George a glance. 'Vanessa's dad could easily have stolen the art and then made it look like we did it by planting evidence. It wouldn't have been too hard for him to get his hands on a key card from our hotel, or a flyer, or a badge.'

Officer Neilsen tapped his fingers against the

bookcase and looked off into the distance as if he was trying to picture all this happening in his head. 'All of that is possible. But why?'

'She's jealous of me,' said Charley triumphantly. 'Plus she's been stealing songs from all over Europe. When we called her out on it, she said she was already working on a way to ruin my career.'

Officer Neilsen stroked his chin. Miss Fairburn looked shocked. Principal Haverstock was holding a piece of croissant halfway between the plate and her mouth.

'Oh!' remembered Charley. 'And she's been posting comments on my Instagram, telling people I'm a criminal!'

Officer Neilsen paused, as if waiting for his close-up. 'I think we need to talk to Vanessa.'

At first no one moved. Then Miss Fairburn jumped to her feet. 'I'll go get her.'

Now *Charley's* stomach was in knots. They were about to find out whether or not Vanessa was behind the crimes after all. Could this be the end of their worries? Could this whole thing be wrapped up in a few moments?

An awkward minute passed. Charley continued to look at her feet, George looked at his dad, and Principal Haverstock looked for croissant crumbs under her desk.

Miss Fairburn returned to the room with Vanessa, who looked like she was ready for attention. When she saw the gathering of people in the room, however, her expression changed to one of confusion.

'Vanessa, we need to ask you a few questions,' said Principal Haverstock softly.

'What's this about?' Vanessa was shaking ever so slightly.

'Are you aware that Charley and George have been linked to some very serious crimes?'

Vanessa looked at Charley, then George, then back to the principal, who said, 'It's OK, Vanessa, you can tell the truth.'

'Yes,' said Vanessa.

'Charley and George seem to think you know a lot about the crimes, and you possibly found out about them before they did. Is that true?'

Vanessa's top lip fluttered, and she swallowed hard. 'Yes,' she said meekly. 'I knew about the crimes.'

'How?' Principal Haverstock had somehow assumed the role of investigator.

Vanessa hesitated. 'My dad's a pilot. He just happened to be in the same cities as Charley and George.'

George glanced at Charley, whose eyes darted up from the floor.

'Go on,' said Principal Haverstock.

Slowly, Vanessa explained. 'When my dad came back from Amsterdam, one of the passengers was the officer in charge of investigating the crime at the Van Gogh Museum. He told my dad about the theft of the painting, and said that he was coming to London to investigate two schoolchildren rockstars about it.'

Officer Neilsen coughed nervously.

'Then, after Charley's show in Rome, the same police officer happened to be on Dad's flight again and told him about the stolen plate.'

All eyes turned towards Officer Neilsen, who had frozen. 'That was your *father*?!' he cried.

'I'm sorry,' interjected Miss Fairburn. 'You talked about the case *with a pilot*?'

Officer Neilsen looked both sheepish and hangdog – sheepdog. 'It was a harmless chat. I didn't know he was the parent of a pupil at the same school the suspects attended.'

There was a moment's pause as everyone took this in.

'Is my dad in trouble?' asked Vanessa softly.

'No,' answered Miss Fairburn. 'And neither are

you. Thank you for being so honest.'

'But, but . . .' started Charley, 'why did you give us the badges?'

'"Senza Pensieri" was going to be my next song,' replied Vanessa. 'I thought if you gave the badges to your fans, they might recognize the phrase when I put my song online.'

'You might wanna check what it means,' said George helpfully.

Vanessa paused before leaving the room, then turned to Charley and George. 'I know I shouldn't have said anything, but you guys have been so mean to me ever since you became rockstars and I just wanted to get back at you.'

'Is that why you keep posting about the crimes on Instagram, Loredana23?' asked Charley quietly.

'Yes,' said Vanessa, blushing. 'I'm sorry about that too.'

★

When the door closed behind Vanessa, George pondered whether they had in fact been mean to her. Were he and Charley the bad guys after all?

He was jolted from his thoughts by a question from Principal Haverstock. 'George, before Charley jumped in, was Vanessa the person you thought was the culprit?'

George knew he didn't have the proof he needed, the final piece of evidence that would confirm his – and Charley's – innocence. But he had no choice. If Charley could be brave, or crazy, enough to name someone, he could be too.

'I think Sam is the culprit,' he said. 'Along with Miss Fairburn.'

DAY 21 – 9.35 a.m.

Rokesbourne High School, LONDON

Even Charley was shocked. She surveyed the room to see her mum aghast, George's dad embarrassed, Sam Mullane outraged and Miss Honor Fairburn horrified. Officer Neilsen stood quietly in the corner, still embarrassed by his previous blunder.

No one spoke for a few seconds, then everyone tried to speak at once. The school bell rang, interrupting the chaos, and the adults in the room instinctively stopped talking. Principal Haverstock used the silence to assume some authority.

'George,' she asked quietly. 'Why do you think Sam

and Miss Fairburn are behind the crimes?'

George reached for his iPad, unlocked the screen and read from his and Charley's case file. 'Sam's the only person we know was definitely at the museums on the same days as Charley and me. Plus he's been mysteriously disappearing in each city.'

Sam's eyes shifted nervously and Charley's mum suddenly sat up straighter in her chair.

George addressed Sam directly. 'In Amsterdam you said you had gone to reception to fix your key card, but you looked like you'd been out all night. Plus how would you know your key card wasn't working if you hadn't left your room?'

He didn't wait for Sam to answer. 'In Rome you said you went for a late-night walk, but you were gone for hours. And in Tours you said you needed to meet the venue owner, Max, the night before the show –'

'I did!' protested Sam.

'But when he saw you the next night,' George continued, 'he said it had been a few years since you'd caught up.'

Sam swallowed hard.

'On top of all this, you somehow came into enough money to buy a new phone.' George hoped all this was enough to prompt a confession.

'So you think I broke into each museum and stole three priceless pieces of art? For a new phone?' asked Sam incredulously.

'Or you got a tour guide to do it for you,' said George. 'We saw you give your number to the guide in Rome, and we saw you chatting to the guide at the chateau.'

'How could I have stolen the art? I didn't even know which bits you were meant to be studying,' protested Sam loudly.

'*You* might not have known,' replied George. 'But Miss Fairburn did. I saw you meeting with her yesterday at the cat cafe.'

Miss Fairburn blushed. Charley's mum tutted.

'And why would Miss Fairburn want to steal the art?' asked Sam, the veins in his temple visibly throbbing.

George glanced at Charley and this time she nodded at him. 'Miss Fairburn needed money for her mother's nursing home,' said George. 'And I overheard her saying she had a plan that involved Charley and me.' He avoided Miss Fairburn's gaze, suddenly feeling ashamed that he had listened in on her conversation.

Officer Neilsen spoke up. 'So are you saying *Sam* accidentally dropped the key card, and the flyer, and the badge?'

George took a deep breath. He knew this was the most serious part of his accusation. 'I think Miss Fairburn and Sam wanted to make it look like Charley and I were the criminals, so they left a clue at each museum. Sam said his key card stopped working in Amsterdam, but maybe he left it at the Van Gogh Museum on purpose.' George looked at his feet. He couldn't face the people he was accusing. 'Miss Fairburn had one of our flyers on her wall, but the day after the theft at the Colosseum it was gone. Maybe she gave it to Sam to plant.'

'But why?' probed Officer Neilsen. 'Didn't Sam have flyers with him?'

'He did,' agreed George, 'but Miss Fairburn wouldn't have known that. Maybe she took one to give to him, but then realized he had a whole stack.'

George knew he was grasping at straws. He would have preferred not to be using so many 'maybes'. Miss Fairburn was ashen-faced. George couldn't tell if she was feeling guilty or betrayed.

Sam glanced around the room, then ran his hand through his thick, dark hair, revealing a few millimetres of grey regrowth. He carefully adjusted the strap on his watch, then addressed the room. What followed was a sentence George had been hoping to hear, but was shocked by nonetheless.

'All right,' said Sam with a look of resignation. 'You caught me.'

This was followed by a sentence George *hadn't* expected.

'I've been gambling,' said Sam.

'What?' George spluttered.

Charley raised her head, Miss Fairburn cocked hers, Charley's mum shook hers, and Sam put his in his hands.

'I'm so sorry,' he yelped. 'I know how hard this industry is and I saw how little money we were actually making after expenses. I just wanted the kids to have something more in the bank than I did when my career ended. I've been going to casinos.'

'So when we saw you in Amsterdam . . .' George prompted.

'I had been out all night at a casino near the Leidseplein.'

'And in Rome?'

'I met up with Sandra, the tour guide, and she took me to a place near the Colosseum. That's why I gave her my number.'

'And that night in Tours?'

'You're right, I didn't go to see Max. I asked the tour guide at the chateau if she knew of anywhere I could place a few bets. She told me about a hotel half an hour from the Old Mill House.'

'Where did you get the money?' Charley's mum was aghast.

Sam swallowed hard. 'I used the cash from the sales of Charley's T-shirts after the shows.'

'That was supposed to go into the children's bank accounts at the end of the tour!' Charley's mum said angrily.

'I know,' said Sam sadly. 'I just thought a few well-placed bets might put a bit more in those accounts. I was going to give it all back.'

'How much did you lose?' asked Charley's mum.

Sam lowered his head and swallowed hard again. 'Well, I made a lot in Amsterdam.' He beamed, then his smile slipped. 'So I, er, used it to buy a new phone!'

The glare he received spoke louder than any words.

'I thought I could use the phone to gamble online and make more money,' Sam said. 'But . . . well, I ended up losing quite a lot. That's why I tried to make some back in Tours.'

Charley's mum spoke again slowly and softly. Somehow it was scarier than when she'd shouted. 'How. Much. Did. You. Lose?'

'All of it,' said Sam, defeated.

'So let me get this right,' said Charley's mum. 'You left the children alone, multiple times, in three different cities, and gambled away all their money?'

'I know,' said Sam. 'I messed up. I'm sorry.'

'Don't apologize to me,' said Charley's mum. 'Apologize to them.'

'I'm sorry,' Sam said, turning to Charley and George. 'I really am.'

Charley's gaze had returned to the floor, and she refused to move it for Sam. Her feelings towards him were pretty clear to everyone in the room.

'You're an idiot,' Charley's mum said.

'I know,' replied Sam meekly. 'But I'm not an art thief.'

George felt angry at Sam for squandering their money, and betrayed by his lies, but he was relieved that Sam hadn't been trying to frame them for an international crime. If Sam wasn't the culprit, though, who was?

'What about Miss Fairburn's plan?' George said. 'And the meeting at the cat cafe?'

'You're right, George,' said Miss Fairburn. 'I did have a plan, but it didn't involve framing you and Charley. I was hoping to convince you to perform a charity concert to raise money for the school. That way we wouldn't have to rely on the inspectors approving our funding. I didn't think it was appropriate to bring it up with you because I'm your teacher, so I talked to Sam instead.'

'But how would a charity concert help you pay for your mother's nursing home?' asked George.

'Well.' Miss Fairburn lowered her eyes. 'I have to admit that it was a bit of a leap. I thought that perhaps the money could go towards establishing a proper theatre here at the school. And that, maybe, I could get a promotion and become the head of performing arts.' Her last sentence came out so fast it sounded like the noise a balloon makes when it's deflating.

'What happened to the flyer then?' asked Charley. 'It wasn't on your wall.'

'I honestly don't know. I just came in one morning and it was gone. I assumed you took it to hand out in Rome.'

George was out of options. Either Vanessa, Sam and Miss Fairburn were all in this together and had come up with the most watertight excuses ever . . . or they were innocent. He knew it was more likely to be the latter. Charley knew it too.

'So what now?' asked Principal Haverstock.

Officer Neilsen took this as his cue. 'Well, I think

it's fair to say that George has not provided me with the culprit. On top of that, we now know that he and Charley were left alone for a significant amount of time in each city, with no one to vouch for their whereabouts. I'm afraid I'll have to place both George and Charley under arrest.'

'What? Why?' Charley's mum and George's dad exclaimed in unison.

'Every bit of evidence points to your children being international art thieves,' answered the officer.

'No!' squealed Charley's mum.

'What does that mean?' asked George's dad as calmly as possible.

'Well,' said the officer, 'the children will be taken in and questioned again about the crimes. And they may be charged with an offence.'

'What's the worst-case scenario?' asked George softly.

The officer pondered the question. 'I guess that would be you going to trial, being found guilty and sentenced to time in a juvenile institution.'

Charley's mum held her heart.

George's dad held Charley's mum's hand. Charley and George held their breath.

'Wait a minute,' said Principal Haverstock. 'This all sounds a bit extreme. They don't need to be sent to prison just yet.'

George flinched at the words 'just yet', but he was still touched by his principal's concern.

'Besides,' she continued, 'we don't want to ruin the school's reputation by making this public. Not until they are proven to be the thieves.'

Ah, thought George. *Of course. It's all about the school's reputation.*

'So what do you suggest?' asked the police officer.

'I'll vouch for the children!' said Principal Haverstock.

'What do you mean?'

'I'll pick them up from their houses each morning, walk them to school and supervise them whenever they aren't in class. Then I'll walk them home at the end of the day to ensure they don't get into any further trouble.'

Charley thought that sounded worse than jail.

'Well, that would be highly unusual . . .' said Officer Neilsen.

'So is divulging the details of an ongoing international police investigation to a member of the public,' replied Principal Haverstock. 'I'm sure your superiors would be very unhappy to hear that little detail.'

Was Principal Haverstock threatening a police officer?

'You can carry on with your investigation while the children stay at school,' she continued in her most principal-like tone. 'If you need to question them, you're more than welcome to do it here in my office. And, in the meantime, you might uncover some clues that prove they didn't steal anything.'

George was both impressed and scared by his principal's tone. The officer seemed to be experiencing the same emotions.

Officer Neilsen stroked his chin, then addressed Charley's and George's parents. 'Can you guarantee the children will be confined to the house during the investigation?'

'Absolutely!' said Charley's mum. George's dad nodded alongside her.

The officer thought for a moment longer. 'All right then,' he said with a sigh. 'But, Charley and George, that means your every spare moment will be spent at home with your parents, or at school with your principal.'

Charley and George shuddered.

'What about the London show?' piped up Sam.

'Oh, I think that will definitely have to be cancelled,' said Officer Neilsen. 'And if I were you I'd cancel the US tour as well. I'm afraid your rockstar days are well and truly done.'

He glanced at Charley's mum and George's dad, and asked, 'Don't you agree?'

Not wanting to contradict the officer who had just allowed their children to avoid being arrested, both parents nodded reluctantly.

George hung his head. Charley whimpered.

The dream was over. It was time to wake up.

LONDON

★ ★ ★

PART 4
LONDON

VIP GUEST

TAXI

LV2 95

Nine days ago, Charley and George were wandering through the gardens of a French chateau, admiring the inventions of Leonardo da Vinci and preparing for a rock show in front of a crowd of mainly adoring fans. Now they sat in a school assembly on a grey and rainy day, surrounded by mainly bored fellow students. Surrounded, but alone.

The days since their last meeting in Principal Haverstock's office had been some of the worst of Charley's life. She used to love the feeling of waking up in her own bed, but not any more. Not only was she forbidden to wake up in any other bed anywhere in the world, she also knew that at exactly 8.35 a.m. Principal Haverstock would arrive, full of fake cheer, to make sure Charley didn't run off and commit a crime on the way to school. They would walk together to George's house, forcing conversation, then collect George and double back towards school.

The whole procedure was humiliating. The jeers of passing students reminded Charley of a picture she'd once seen, of someone in medieval times with their head stuck through a hole in a plank of wood, getting rotten fruit thrown at them. She wondered if that would have been less embarrassing than walking to school with your principal. And eating lunch with your principal. And spending every single break time with your principal.

To make matters worse, today was supposed to have been the big homecoming show in London. A statement had been released saying that the show had been cancelled 'for logistical reasons', which had sent the Rokesbourne rumour mill into hyperdrive.

'I heard the audience walked out halfway through one of her shows.'

'Apparently she threw a tantrum in the dressing room when someone brought her the wrong chocolate bar.'

'It's not even her voice. She just lip-syncs to a backing track.'

In one way, sitting in the school assembly was a relief. After a week of being mocked, laughed at and lied about, Charley and George were happy to be out of the spotlight for a moment. Unfortunately Principal Haverstock had other ideas.

'I'm sorry to tell you that Charley Parker and George Carling won't be touring any more,' she announced to every single member of the school. 'But, on the upside, it does mean they're back with us full-time!'

Presumably she was trying to put a positive spin on the situation, but the announcement was met with a cacophony of gasps and murmurs, and even a few sniggers. A wave of noise rose and every head turned towards Charley and George, who were well and truly back in centre stage.

As the assembly ended, Principal Haverstock added insult to injury. 'OK, students, since it's almost break time, let's end assembly early. You can all have an extra five minutes of freedom.'

Cheers followed.

'Except for Charley and George. You two stay here for the moment, and I'll take you back to my office.'

Laughter followed.

The former rockstars stayed in place as the entire school filed past. Many words were thrown their way, but Charley managed to ignore them all. For possibly the first time ever, Vanessa passed by without saying anything, but her bandmate Tara stopped.

'I'm really sorry your tour didn't work out. I think you're really talented,' she mumbled, before scurrying away.

Charley's steely veneer started to crack. Tears formed in her eyes. She thought back to the Too Cool for School competition and remembered how she had resisted entering because she didn't want to be humiliated in front of the school. Now her nightmare had come true.

'Right then,' said Principal Haverstock once the pupils and teachers had dispersed. 'Ready to spend another break time together?'

The nightmare was getting worse.

★

DAY 25 – 11.15 a.m.
Rokesbourne High School, LONDON

Charley and George sat alone in Principal Haverstock's office. It was the last place they wanted to be and yet it was the only place they wouldn't be ridiculed.

'I just have to photocopy some files for the school inspectors,' said the principal in a gratingly chirpy voice. 'I'll be right outside, so don't do anything I wouldn't do.' She paused. 'Like stealing a priceless painting.'

Unaware of the comedy stink bomb she'd let off, the principal trotted from the room, leaving Charley and George on their own for the first time since the Old Mill House.

A tense silence sat between them, like an enormous awkward elephant. It was hard to believe that only a couple of weeks ago they had been best buddies. As the seconds ticked past, the elephant shifted uncomfortably in its seat. Something had to be said.

In the end, Charley and George said the same thing at the same time: 'I'm sorry.'

Then George said, 'I'd like to go first, if that's OK.' Charley didn't object, so he ploughed on. 'I'm sorry I told Officer Neilsen we'd crack the case. I was just trying to buy some time so you could do your show.'

'That's OK.' Charley gave George a sad smile. 'I'm sorry I froze you out. I just didn't know how to deal with all this, so I kinda shut down.'

'I understand. I really thought we were going to find the culprit,' George said ruefully.

'Me too,' said Charley. 'Maybe if I hadn't shut

you out after the show in Tours we could have put our heads together and worked it out.'

'And maybe if I hadn't given us an impossible deadline we'd have had time to investigate properly.'

Charley paused. 'We've got time now.'

George paused too. 'Go on then.'

Charley picked up her bag and shuffled her seat towards George. George picked up his backpack and extricated his iPad. The elephant picked up its trunk and left the room.

George opened a new note, typed the words 'WHO DID IT?' at the top and sat back in his chair. 'So what do we know about the thief? Instead of focusing on suspects, let's look at the evidence.'

Charley agreed. 'Whoever it was must have been able to access a key card from our hotel in Amsterdam.'

'That wouldn't have been hard,' said George. 'They kept a whole stack of them behind reception. Anyone could've sneaked back there and grabbed one.'

'True. But not many people had access to our flyers. Unless Sam handed some out. Or one fell out of your backpack.' George was about to protest, but Charley explained, 'I'm just covering all possibilities.'

'What about the badges?' said George. 'Did I drop one of those as well?'

'Maybe,' said Charley. 'Although I did give one to the tour guide. Maybe she dropped it. Or gave it away.'

'But to who?' George thought out loud. 'It had to be someone who knew which pieces of art we had to study.'

'Not necessarily,' said Charley. 'All along we've thought that we were sent to the art that someone was already planning to steal. But what if we were looking at it the wrong way round? Someone could have followed us, seen what pieces of art we spent time looking at, then stolen those pieces – and planted evidence to make it look like we were the thieves.'

'But who would do that?'

'Well, we know Ruby was following us in Rome,' said Charley. 'Perhaps she was in Amsterdam too, but we just didn't notice her.'

'Hang on, what are you saying?' asked George.

'I'm not saying anything for sure, but I am asking something. Could Ruby Sherring have somehow got hold of a key card in Amsterdam, a flyer in Rome and a badge in Tours?'

'It's definitely possible,' said George.

'Could she have followed us to each museum, seen which pieces we studied, then planted evidence to make us look like the thieves?'

'It's not *im*possible,' said George.

'And could she have persuaded a staff member to help her steal valuable pieces of art?'

'Well, she won *us* over pretty quickly.' George frowned.

From the hallway came the sound of Principal Haverstock humming happily to herself.

'Hang on,' said George. 'If Ruby is the thief, then that means she lied about what happened at the chateau.'

'Yes,' confirmed Charley.

'It would also mean that we actually gave her the perfect opportunity to steal something.'

'Yes,' repeated Charley. 'And maybe when we told her that the *Mona Lisa* was a copy, she decided to steal a notebook instead. Or . . . or maybe she chose the notebook because she knew *we* knew *she* knew –' Charley pulled a face at this mouthful – 'we were expecting the thief to steal the *Mona Lisa*, and she thought the notebook would make her seem even less likely as a suspect.'

'I just can't believe Ruby would lie to us,' said George doubtfully.

'Well, she lied to us about working at *M Magazine*,' Charley pointed out. 'If only there was a way of finding out if Ruby was in Amsterdam . . .'

'Maybe there is.' George paused, listening to the sounds coming from outside the office door. When he was confident that both Principal Haverstock and the photocopier were still happily humming, he tapped the screen to open his videos, then the file named 'Amsterdam'.

'I doubt she was at our show,' said Charley.

'You're probably right,' admitted George, 'but it couldn't hurt to check. You never know what we might find.'

As the video loaded . . . and loaded . . . and loaded . . . Charley finally took note of the song Principal Haverstock was humming.

'Turns out it *was* a catchy tune after all,' she said to George with a wistful smile.

'I told you. But you were right. The lyrics would have made a much better comedy routine.'

Charley and George looked at each other, their brains whirring. Charley's eyes widened, George's eyes narrowed, and they both started to say something when George's iPad made a sound. The video had finally begun to play.

Charley peered over George's shoulder, staring intently at the screen and scanning the footage of the crowd. The faces in the darkness reminded Charley of the crazy, wonderful life she had lived only a few weeks ago.

'There!' George pointed at the screen.

'Zoom in!'

George enlarged the image, and they looked at each other in amazement. This time Charley's eyes narrowed and George's eyes widened.

'It's her!' cried Charley. 'I don't believe it!'

'I do,' said George, with what was probably the biggest smile ever. 'I think we just cracked the case!'

'Not quite yet,' said Charley. 'Let's do what we should have done last time: put our heads together over the weekend, collect all the evidence we possibly can, then present a rock-solid case at a meeting on Monday morning.'

'Good call.' George grinned.

'We've got this.' Charley nodded. 'We've totally got this.'

Charley and George entered Principal Haverstock's office with their heads held high. Even though they'd been confined to their own houses, they'd spent the entire weekend working together. Text messages, video chats and evidence files were exchanged, and by the time they awoke on Monday morning, they were *pretty sure* they had everything they needed to prove their innocence, save their careers and identify the true culprit.

They were the last to enter the room on purpose – for dramatic effect, but also so they could have one final conversation in the hallway. Already seated were

Charley's mum and George's dad, Sam (who was talking to an expert about his gambling problem), Miss Fairburn (who had forgiven them for their previous accusation) and Principal Haverstock (who looked entirely bored with the whole affair).

Also in the room was a red-haired girl with a nose piercing, Ruby Sherring, who nodded at Charley and George as they entered. The two detectives had insisted on Ruby's presence, saying they wanted an official journalist to record the proceedings. Officer Neilsen had begrudgingly agreed, and he now stood pensively in the corner.

'We know who the thief is,' said Charley, full of confidence. 'And it is somebody in this room.' She was enjoying the moment, as was George.

'Who is it this time?' Principal Haverstock was annoyed. 'One of your parents? Or are you going to tell us Officer Neilsen did it?'

'Neither.' George grinned. He glanced round the room, from Sam to Miss Fairburn, to his dad, to Charley's mum, to Officer Neilsen. Finally his eyes landed on Ruby, who was now quite jittery.

George held Ruby's gaze for a second, then turned to face Principal Haverstock. 'It was you.'

The room fell completely silent.

Principal Haverstock was stunned. 'Me?' she cried. 'That's the most ridiculous thing I've ever heard in my life. This meeting is over.'

'Let the children finish,' said Officer Neilsen calmly. 'I want to hear their reasoning.'

Charley and George took the floor. Everyone in the room stared at them, desperate to hear what they would say next.

'Last Friday,' said Charley, 'while Principal Haverstock was outside this very room copying files, she hummed one of my tunes – a new song by the name of "Smells Like Home". At first I took it as a compliment, but then I realized I had only performed that song once, on stage in Tours. And it went so badly that we didn't put the video online.'

She looked at George, who continued, 'Which meant the only way Principal Haverstock could have heard the song was if she had been in the audience of the show in Tours.'

'Fine,' said their principal crossly. 'You caught me. I took a day off school to come and see my favourite students do their last-ever show. That's hardly a crime.'

'Is that why you were eating a croissant when we had our last meeting?' asked Charley innocently.

'What?'

'A croissant. You apologized when you arrived late, saying you hadn't had time for any breakfast. You'd brought a croissant with you. Did you bring some home from France?'

'I – well, yes, as a matter of fact,' answered Principal Haverstock warily.

'That's exactly what we thought,' said Charley. 'But that got us thinking more. When we came back from Amsterdam, you were eating a biscuit.'

'So?' The principal sounded like a petulant five-year-old.

'But it wasn't any old biscuit,' said George. 'It was a stroopwafel. The kind you often find in Holland.' He held up his iPad to show a photograph of Melly's Stroopwafels (with the S added to make it SMelly's).

'And when we came back from Rome,' said Charley, 'you were eating pastries filled with chocolate. Pastries commonly found in the cafes of Italy, known as cannoli.'

Again George held up his screen, this time displaying a photo of cannoli. They were an exact match for the tubular snack Principal Haverstock had devoured in the room only a few weeks ago.

'This doesn't prove anything,' protested the principal.

'True,' said Charley. 'But it made us wonder if

perhaps you had come to those shows as well. Luckily we were searching for footage of the audience in Amsterdam when we heard you humming in the hallway. And look what we found.'

George pressed play on the next file and images of the Dutch audience appeared on screen. He let it play for a few seconds then paused and zoomed in.

Most of the faces of Charley's fans were in darkness, but something stood out. Something bright, something fluorescent, something familiar – a Rokesbourne High School lanyard, holding a teacher's ID card.

George zoomed in further to reveal the name on the ID: Principal Victoria Haverstock.

Miss Fairburn suddenly spoke up. 'All those days you said you were meeting the school inspectors, you were actually going to Charley and George's shows!'

All eyes turned again to the principal, who was suddenly pale but defiant. 'Yes, I went to the shows. But only to make sure you didn't do anything on stage that would endanger the school's reputation! We can't risk losing any more funding.' Looking around the room, Principal Haverstock decided to double down. 'I didn't steal any art. And unless you can prove I did there will be serious consequences.'

What could be worse than being chaperoned every day by

your own principal? thought Charley.

'I'm curious,' interjected Officer Neilsen. 'How do you think your principal actually carried out the thefts?'

George took the lead. 'I'm glad you asked. It occurred to us that wearing a lanyard to a concert was quite an unusual thing to do. Unless someone wanted to look official. In fact, I once thought that Principal Haverstock's lanyard made her look so official that she could probably walk into a hospital and people would let her start operating.'

There was a small ripple of laughter, and George took a moment to enjoy it before pressing on. 'If that was the case, she could probably walk into a museum and take a piece of art, and, as long as she looked calm and confident, people would assume she worked there. They'd think she was a staff member taking something away to be stored or cleaned.'

Charley's mum nodded. So did George's dad. Sam looked confused.

'And if you can fix a leaky ceiling with some gaffer tape on the end of a hockey stick,' said Charley to her principal, 'you could easily cover the lens of a CCTV camera the same way.'

'These are all unfounded claims.' Principal Haverstock rose to her feet. 'Fanciful theories with no evidence behind them. Unless you've got more, I think we're done here.'

Officer Neilsen remained in place. So did Miss Fairburn. And Sam, and Charley's mum, and George's dad.

'We do have more,' said Charley. 'When we left the chateau in France, someone stayed behind to keep an eye out for anything suspicious.' Charley indicated Ruby. 'Ruby told us she saw a tour guide near the notebooks, but she didn't pay them much attention. However, when the chateau closed, Ruby sat in her car for the night and watched on. When the tour guides left for the evening, she studied them in case anyone looked suspicious.'

George took over, wheeling towards Ruby. 'Do you remember what those tour guides looked like?' he asked, knowing full well how she was going to answer.

'Yes,' said Ruby.

'And is one of them in this room right now?' asked Charley, remembering Ruby's nod when they had entered the room.

'Yes,' said Ruby.

'And could you please point to the person you saw leaving the chateau on the night the notebook was stolen?'

Slowly and firmly, Ruby pointed at Principal Haverstock, who opened her mouth to speak. Nothing came out.

'You, Principal Haverstock,' said Charley, 'have been following George and me around Europe, stealing valuable pieces of art from museums while pretending to be a staff member, and planting evidence to make it look like we did it. You took a key card from the hotel in Amsterdam, stole the flyer from Miss Fairburn's wall to drop in Rome and left behind the badge we gave you at the chateau.'

All faces were turned to the school principal. They awaited her response, but once again she seemed unable to make a noise. The only sound was a slow, steady round of applause. Officer Neilsen was clapping and nodding his head.

'OK,' said Principal Haverstock weakly. 'You caught me. I am the thief.' She stood and faced the window, surveying the students outside. 'I do a lot for this school, and I receive very little help. We rely on every bit of funding we can scrape together. Doors have fallen off hinges, windows are cracked, books are torn and ripped.' She turned back to the room. 'But I can't fix any of them if we don't meet certain standards. Decent facilities. Good results. Perfect attendance. The three Rs: repairs, reputation, records.'

The principal directed her next words at Charley and George. 'We barely satisfy any of these criteria, and your days off to do shows in Europe have put our funding in jeopardy. If you tour the US next year, we won't meet the attendance levels. Which means we won't qualify for funding.'

Charley's mum interjected angrily. 'So you sabotaged the children's tour?'

'I did it to save the school! To stop us being merged with Queenswood High.' Principal Haverstock had tears in her eyes. 'I thought I could make it look like you were connected to the missing art,' she said to Charley and George. 'But I didn't want you to get in trouble. I just wanted it to look suspicious

enough that your parents would stop you from touring.'
She took a deep breath. 'So I asked Miss Fairburn to
assign you a piece of art to study at each destination. I
found out what the artwork was, either by asking Miss
Fairburn or by lurking nearby when you were discussing
it. Then, after you had visited each museum, I waited
until closing time and I took the museum pieces. You're
right, George. When you're wearing a lanyard, people
assume you know what you're doing.'

'But how did you get the art out of the museums?'
asked Officer Neilsen, trying desperately to do his job.

'I didn't,' answered Principal Haverstock. 'I hid the
Van Gogh piece in a cupboard and the Roman plate in
a locker. The *Mona Lisa* was too big to hide, so I took
one of da Vinci's notebooks and hid it in the bedroom,
under his chamber pot. I thought you'd find them after
a little while. I never had any intention of taking the
art for myself. And I didn't think Charley and George
would actually be arrested for theft, because technically
nothing was ever stolen.'

Everyone turned to Officer Neilsen who, it must be
said, was not nailing this case. First he had given away
key details of the thefts to a stranger, now it transpired
he had missed vital, and fairly obvious, clues – namely,
the missing art, which apparently had never actually

been missing at all.

'In fact,' continued Principal Haverstock, directly to the officer, 'this would have all been over sooner if you had hadn't waited three hours to check the key card in Amsterdam. I had an extra one made up for Charley's room.'

'How?' asked Charley.

Principal Haverstock waved her lanyard in the air.

'I went to reception and told them a guest called Charley Parker had lost her card and needed a new one. They assumed I worked there and made a new one on the spot. I thought that would be enough for your parents to call off the tour.'

Officer Neilsen gave an embarrassed cough.

'When the Amsterdam theft wasn't enough, I took the plate in Rome,' continued the principal. 'When your parents *still* didn't stop the tour, I had to go to the chateau.'

'Why didn't you just *talk* to us?' asked Charley's mum.

'It wouldn't have worked,' retorted Principal Haverstock. 'Parents always think their children's dreams are more important than their education.'

Charley's mum was livid. George's dad was horrified. Sam wasn't quite sure why he was there, and

Ruby was taking notes.

'I'm sorry I almost ruined your careers, Charley and George,' Principal Haverstock continued sadly. 'If it's any consolation, I think I have ruined my own. I just wanted to do what was right for the school.'

There was a beat as everyone in the room processed what they had just heard.

'So now what do we do?' asked Sam.

'I've got an idea,' said Charley, giving George a wink.

CHARLEY P INSTAGRAM VIDEO

♡ ◯ ∘∘∘   ⇒

'London is on!'
131,504 views

Top comments
FlorenceC Yes!!!! So excited the London
show is back on! See you there!!! Xxx

Karin N My dad said he'd take me to London for the show!!!

Loredana23 O M actual G, you guys. Charley P is innocent! Someone was setting her up the whole time. I heard it yesterday. We should totally get behind her and support her as much as we can. #FreeCharleyP

> **LeilaToomler** Now I wish I hadn't burned her shirt. Oh well, I guess I'll just have to buy another one.
>
> **MayZee** Someone tried to frame Charley and George? What a loser.

DAY 40 – *3.05 p.m.*
Rokesbourne High School, LONDON

Charley Parker and George Carling looked out at the sea of people in front of them. From their vantage point at the side of the stage, they could see every single beaming face in the crowd. George had initially been worried about doing an outdoor concert in London in winter, but the gods of British weather had blessed them with one of those clear but crisp sunny Saturdays.

'When you do a good thing with the right intention, the universe will reward you,' said Charley with a new-found sense of calm.

In the days that had followed Principal Haverstock's

confession, Charley had made a list of what she had learned throughout the whole ordeal:

1 I am capable.

2 People can do bad things with good intentions.

3 Sometimes it's better to work as part of a team. In fact, it's almost always better to work as a team.

The first lesson was a particularly important one, because it stopped Charley doubting her own abilities. When things had got tough during the investigation, Charley had lost all hope that she and George could solve the crimes. And yet between them they'd managed to do what a police officer couldn't.

The second lesson applied to Sam and Principal Haverstock in particular. They had each made a misstep, but that didn't necessarily make them bad people. In fact, they were both trying to do the right thing in the wrong way. This led Charley to the conclusion that the best course of action was to do good things for good reasons.

The third lesson, of course, applied to Charley and George. In fact, that was why Miss Fairburn had suggested they study the painting of the boots, and Septimius's sons, and the *Mona Lisa*. What had made the painting so famous? Was it the painter or the model? The answer, of course, was both. The combination of da Vinci's skill and the model's aura made the painting one of the most famous in the world. In much the same way, when Charley and George worked together, they were unstoppable.

Those three lessons had led Charley to her grand idea.

'George and I will do a concert, just like Miss Fairburn suggested,' she'd announced in Principal Haverstock's office. 'We'll do it in the schoolyard on a weekend and all ticket sales will be donated directly to the school.'

Sam had lifted his head to raise an objection but quickly thought better of it.

'If we do it properly, we'll raise enough money to fix the doors, buy new books and maybe even upgrade the performing-arts facilities.'

'I think that's a great idea,' Miss Fairburn replied. 'Although I do have one suggestion.'

Now, standing alongside each other at the side of

the stage, Charley and George had to agree it was a pretty good suggestion. Neither of them would have considered asking Vanessa and Devine Intervention to be their supporting act for the charity concert, but, watching the band in action, they were glad Miss Fairburn had.

Dexter Keaton, the recent winner of the Too Cool for School competition, had kicked off the show with his mix of rap and magic. He asked the crowd if they wanted him to drop some Eminem, then he somehow made it rain M&M's from his magician's hat. That's right – he actually pulled a rapper out of his hat.

'Are you ready?' asked Miss Fairburn, who had recently assumed the title (and increased salary) of Acting Principal.

'I am,' replied Charley. 'What about you, George?'

It had been Charley's idea for George to perform a short stand-up set right before she went on stage. If she could believe in herself as a rockstar and a detective, then it was about time George believed in himself as a stand-up comic.

'Sure am,' said George tentatively. He glanced down at a number of comedy topics written on his hand. The first was 'Smells Like Home'.

The last notes of 'Senza Pensieri' rang out across the

schoolyard, and Vanessa signed off with an exuberant 'Thank you, Rokesbourne!' She bounded off stage, crossing paths with Miss Fairburn, and headed towards Charley and George.

'Thank you,' she said to Charley, then looked at George and added, 'Follow that!'

'I'll do my best.' George grinned.

On stage, Miss Fairburn took the microphone and thanked Devine Intervention for their performance. Charley scanned the crowd for familiar faces. Her mum was there, of course, as were George's parents. Sam was at the very back of the schoolyard, doing a head count and miserably calculating how much money they would have made were they not donating it all to the school.

Off to the side, Charley spied Principal Haverstock. It was clear she could no longer continue to run the school, and she had voluntarily resigned, but she had been saved from a jail sentence by the fact that nothing had actually been stolen. When Officer Neilsen had hinted that Principal Haverstock could be charged with causing a public mischief, Charley had pointed out that *he* could be accused of bungling the investigation. Neilsen's eventual report stated that the missing pieces had been 'relocated' by some 'cleaners' and that the whole thing had been a 'misunderstanding'.

With George taking the stage, Ruby had offered to stand in as camera operator for the show. She'd positioned herself in George's old spot – offstage and to the left. Charley and George kept their promise to give Ruby the story of the thefts, but not for a magazine article. If the details of the case ever went public, both Principal Haverstock and Officer Neilsen would be humiliated – and nobody wanted that. Instead they suggested that Ruby turn the whole thing into a movie script. After all, she had said she wanted to be a screenwriter.

Ruby agreed, but she also went ahead with her original feature about music in the age of social media. She submitted it to the editor of *M Magazine*, who liked the article so much that he put Charley and George on the front cover with the headline: 'TikTok! Times Are Changing for the Music Industry'.

There was one face in particular that Charley was searching for in the crowd and she spotted it in the front row. It was the face of Officer Neilsen's daughter. According to Officer Neilsen, his daughter had been convinced all along that Charley and George were innocent, which was why he hadn't arrested them in Tours.

Charley waved to catch her attention, then blew a kiss. The young girl exploded with joy, then cuddled her father tightly.

'Hey,' said George hesitantly. 'Do you think if my comedy spot goes well, I could be your support act when we tour the US?'

'Absolutely!' said Charley. 'I'd love that.'

'I'm so glad the tour's back on,' said George. He was nervous, excited, panicky and feeling strangely at home – all at the same time.

'Me too,' said Charley. 'And I'm glad we're taking tutors with us. This concert might take care of repairs and reputation, but we've got to keep up our records. The three Rs are still covered!'

Miss Fairburn was rambling into the microphone now, caught up in the occasion, but it allowed Charley and George to finish their conversation.

'The only R we need now is some rest,' joked George.

'Thank goodness this is the last show before Christmas,' said Charley. 'I need a break.'

'Yeah,' said George. 'Me too. But I reckon we'll bounce back bigger and better next year.'

'You said it,' replied Charley. She offered her fist for him to bump. George responded with a high five, then wrapped his hand over Charley's.

'It's almost time to see Charley P,' said Miss Fairburn. 'But first, please welcome Rokesbourne's very own George Carling!'

'You know what?' said George, looking at Charley. 'I've got a feeling next year is gonna be our best one yet.'

'I agree,' said Charley. 'What could possibly go wrong?'

TIKTOK!
TIMES ARE CHANGING FOR THE MUSIC INDUSTRY

by Ruby Sherring

Millions of years ago, dinosaurs ruled the earth. They walked unchallenged, every other being cowering in their wake. Then one day a meteorite fell from the sky, a shooting star, and their world changed forever. The dinosaurs could no longer survive in their new environment and they became extinct.

Today a different type of dinosaur is in danger of extinction. But this time it's not due to one star. It's due to hundreds, maybe thousands. The music industry is changing and the days of the cigar-smoking, power-hungry record executives might soon be over.

Charley P is one of a new breed of stars who have bypassed record labels, radio programmers and publicity companies to take their music to the world, and the world seems to like it. Together with her social media guru, George Carling, Charley has used the internet to showcase her talents directly to her peers, using the most powerful form of publicity there is – word of mouth.

Don't worry if you've never heard of them – your children probably have. Not only that, they've probably interacted with them on Facebook, followed them on Instagram and watched them on TikTok. Charley P isn't a star despite you not knowing who she is; she's a star *because* you don't know who she is.

Charley (and George) exist independently of the machinations of big business, and connect directly to their fans, in much the same way that your kids want to exist independently of you and connect directly to their heroes.

Today's music stars aren't being discovered by talent scouts, A&R reps or PR bosses; they're being discovered by their fans. There's no need for a middleman, let alone a middle-aged man. The environment has changed, and these new stars have the world at their fingertips. Literally.

With a few taps on George's iPad, Charley P can announce a concert in the US, sell merchandise in Denmark and post a photo from Ireland – all within a few minutes. And, if you're wondering whether there's actually a 'grown-up' behind this clever marketing, I can assure you there isn't. Not only that, from what I've seen, this new generation can handle just about anything – on stage and off.

So look out, music dinosaurs, your world is already changing. It's up to you how you adapt – because more shooting stars are coming, whether you like it or not.

ACKNOWLEDGEMENTS

I know everyone thanks their editors at this point, but I REALLY want to thank mine. Thank you Natalie for seeing the potential in this story, and for pointing it in the right direction. Thank you Ruth for polishing off the rough edges, reshaping it, and suggesting alterations, until the rough lump of clay I threw down that vaguely resembled a bowl eventually turned into quite a detailed piece of work. Thank you again to Natalie who returned to the fray and applied the invaluable finishing touches. On top of that, thank you to all the various editors who cast their gaze across it, especially Pippa, who oversaw them all.

An ENORMOUS Thank you to Luna, who brought Charley and George to life in a way that made me get to know them better, and to Ben for his stellar design work. To all at Penguin and Puffin, thank you for taking a punt on a comedian with an idea.

To the Australian Government, thank you for introducing hotel quarantine measures that saw me locked in a room for two 14-day stretches, with no alternative but to write.

Thank you to my agents Joe and Rich, for humouring me when I said I had an idea for a book.

Thank you to my wife, for giving compliments when I most needed them.

And thank you to my two wonderful daughters. I've come to realise that you embody the best characteristics of Charley and George. Or they embody the best characteristics of you. Smart, funny, stylish, and capable. In particular, thank you Beatrice for saying you wanted to be a Rockstar and a Detective one day. I literally wouldn't have written this book without you.